THE
DRAGON'S
CHILD

A STORY OF ANGEL ISLAND

THE DRAGON'S CHILD

A STORY OF ANGEL ISLAND

LAURENCE YEP

with

DR. KATHLEEN S. YEP

HarperCollins*Publishers*

*To my father, Yep Gim Lew, who made
the long journey, and to my grandfather Yep Lung Gon,
who made the journey again and again.*
—L.Y.

*To my grandparents, Yep Gim Lew,
Franche Yep, and Lee Sun Ngan,
for making this book possible.*
—K.S.Y.

The Dragon's Child
Text copyright © 2008 by Laurence Yep
www.harpercollinschildrens.com
Library of Congress Cataloging-in-Publication Data
Yep, Laurence, 1948-
  The dragon's child : a story of Angel Island / Laurence Yep and Dr. Kathleen S. Yep. — 1st
ed.
      p.   cm.
  Summary: In 1922, ten-year-old Gim Lew reluctantly leaves his village in China to accom-
pany his father to America, but before they go he must prepare for a grueling test that he must
pass—without stuttering—at California's Angel Island, where strict officials strive to keep out
unwanted immigrants. Includes facts about immigration from China and the experiences of
the author's family.
  Includes bibliographical references.
  ISBN 978-0-06-027692-8 (trade bdg.) — ISBN 978-0-06-027693-5 (lib. bdg.)
  [1. Emigration and immigration—Fiction. 2. Fathers and sons—Fiction.
3. Chinese Americans—Fiction. 4. Stuttering—Fiction. 5. China—History—1912-1928—
Fiction. 6. Angel Island (Calif.)—History—20th century—Fiction. 7. California—
History—1850–1950—Fiction.] I. Yep, Kathleen S. II. Title.
PZ7.Y44Amt 2008   2007018373
[Fic]—dc22   CIP
                                                                            AC
Typography by Christopher Stengel
1 2 3 4 5 6 7 8 9 10
❖
First Edition

Contents

Author's Note

How many people have a chance to travel back in time to meet their grandparents when they were children? That's exactly the prospect my niece Dr. Kathleen S. Yep presented to me when she found the transcripts of the immigration interview of her grandfather, my father.

The interviews with my father, my uncles, and my own grandfather (Kathleen's grandfather, great-uncles, and great-grandfather) cover some five hundred pages and are accompanied by photos going back to 1887. Among other things, I was surprised to read that my grandfather had been born in San Francisco in 1868 (the transcontinental railroad was to be completed a year later), making him an early native-born Chinese American. I also learned that after one of his visits to China, he returned to San Francisco a day after the Great Earthquake of 1906. I wonder what he must have seen when he arrived in a city in ruins, with the Great Fire destroying what had survived the earthquake.

My grandfather lived in San Francisco for the first thirteen years of his life, watching the city change as the newly constructed railroad brought people from the rest of America. Then he and his parents returned to China. When he was eighteen, he married a woman named Wong Shee. His father died at about the same time, and his mother died a year afterward. A year later, after fathering the first of his many children, my grandfather returned to America, where he was to spend most of the rest of his life. Like many other Chinese American men, he left his family in China but visited them often.

The U.S. immigration officials wanted to make sure that the Chinese man who left America was the same one who was trying to come back. The officials conducted lengthy, detailed interrogations about the traveler's village and his journeys back and forth. Transcripts of the interviews were kept on each traveler. After several trips, a traveler like my grandfather would have a thick folder full of paperwork.

Because my grandfather had been born in America, his children, including my father, were also American citizens—even though they were born and raised in China. When my uncles came to join my grandfather in America, their interviews filled even more folders.

As I looked at the transcripts, I began to see their Chinese village and the surrounding fields emerge. And when my grandfather finally brought my father from China to America, I saw a new image of my father. I had known my father as an energetic shopkeeper and vigorous athlete, but from his interview I now saw him as a small boy.

Though he fought no warriors and killed no monsters, my father's journey to America is no less courageous in its own small, personal way. Nor do I think my father was an exception. Most other immigrants did not face the legal obstacles Chinese immigrants faced (some of which are described in the afterword). But courage is something they all shared, for it was not easy to uproot yourself from the familiar and make the often dangerous trip to these shores.

Though this book is a work of fiction, it is based on facts drawn from the immigration files, as well as on my own research. But historical fiction is more than a record of dates and statistics: it should be a dialogue with the dead. And so this novel is a conversation with my father about his long journey to Angel Island and America.

The Secret

QUESTION: *What was life like in China?*

POP: *When I was little, I used my left hand and not my right. So I got hit for using the wrong hand. And that kind of made me nervous, and when that happened I stuttered a little bit. That made people even madder.*

March 7, 1922
Ninth day of the second month,
eleventh year of the Chinese Republic
Lung Hing Village, Southern China

My father was a dragon. Lung Gon was his name. And he came from a village of dragons.

But I wasn't the least bit like him.

When I forgot myself, I naturally used my left hand.

I kept forgetting to use my right hand. That was the correct one.

There were a lot of practical reasons for me to use my right hand. For one thing, I wouldn't bump whoever sat next to me at the dinner table and make him drop his rice bowl. Some superstitious folk thought left-handed people were sneaky. A few even swore it brought bad luck when you used your left hand.

But when I used my right hand, I had trouble writing. My brushstrokes went all over the page. When I used my left hand, the words came out fine. Only I couldn't do that. I had to remind myself to use my right hand all the time.

The winter rains had let up, but the air still felt damp. Everyone felt drowsy that afternoon. The New Year's celebrations had tired our little village. Even my teacher, Uncle Jing, was droning more slowly than usual.

I thought it was safe to use my left hand to write with while Uncle Jing's back was turned. But then a fly buzzed around his head. When he twisted to swat it, he saw me.

I knew what would happen next. It was as sure to come as a sunrise, and as sure as our rooster crowing at that sunrise.

"You must always write with your right hand!" Uncle Jing scolded in his shrill voice. "You're the son and brother of Guests! Do you think any of them do such an awful thing?" He always taught with a bamboo rod in his hand. It began to twitch eagerly, like a dog's tail.

No one ever let me forget that I was the son of a Guest of the Golden Mountain—or America, as the people there called it.

Most of the time I spoke clearly. But when I got nervous, I stuttered sometimes. Before I recited a lesson, I always rehearsed it like an actor. And I had to keep telling myself to stay calm. However, I would get so worried that I stammered even more.

If I stuttered at school, my classmates would laugh and Uncle would get mad and hit me. If I did it at home, Mother would scold me. Sister would look disappointed and tell me to try harder.

I had finally gotten to meet my father two years earlier, when I was seven. He had brought my older brother Yuen home to get married. Father had told me at that time that I shouldn't stutter anymore. But it seemed the more I tried not to think about stammering, the more my tongue tripped. Even though my father and Yuen had gone back to America, I still tried to obey him.

"I'm s-s-sorry," I barely managed to say to Uncle. "I f-f-forgot."

The rest of the class rocked back and forth with laughter. Of all the students, I was the only pupil from my clan, even though the school was our village's. My brothers and cousins had all left to find work overseas. The five other students came from neighboring villages. Two of them didn't own desks, so they sat on the dirt floor.

"What did your father tell you about stuttering and using your left hand?" he huffed.

I didn't say anything. I didn't trust my tongue.

Uncle Jing answered his own question. "He'll blame me when you're the one being stubborn and willful. One stroke!" The bamboo tipped in a slow circle, as if Uncle was loosening up his arm. "Put out your hand."

I heard a commotion from one end of the village. Uncle and the rest of the class were too involved with anticipating the beating to notice.

Miserable, I extended my hand across the desk. Over many years, the wood had soaked up the fragrance of all the ink spilled on it. The desk belonged to my family. At the end of the term, old Dip Shew would have to carry it home to our house. He was a poor cousin we had hired to take care of our fields.

Uncle's fingers brushed the back of my neck. He was still used to reaching for a boy's queue. In the old days when the savage Manchus had taken over China, they made all Chinese males wear their hair in long queues. The queues were a symbol of the tails of the horses the Manchus had ridden when they conquered us. Now that

4

the Manchus had been driven away, we didn't have to wear our hair long. Now there wasn't anything to grab.

I made the mistake of smiling.

"Five more for being insolent!" Uncle yelled.

Whoosh!

The bamboo rod swished through the air. The pain lashed my hand, but I bit my lip. The other boys were grinning. I couldn't expect any sympathy from them. They always liked it when I got punished, even though I had never done anything to them. They disliked me because my family was rich from the money Father and my brothers sent home.

Whoosh!

Uncle hit me even harder this time. I think he wanted to see tears.

I wouldn't give him the satisfaction.

Whoosh!

My sister appeared in the doorway. "Excuse me," she said. Sister was eleven years older than me and had practically raised me; Mother had been busy with all our family affairs. "Father's home."

Uncle straightened up as if he'd just been whacked himself. "He's not due back for another week."

Sister raised her eyebrows as if to ask what I had done now. But she stepped hastily into the room to come to my rescue. She was always doing that. "His boat came in

5

early. My mother wants my brother." She pulled me away from the desk and Uncle's bamboo rod.

Uncle squirmed for a moment, and then he laid his precious bamboo rod down on his desk. "Well," he harrumphed, "since it's such a happy occasion, we'll forget the other three strokes." He clasped his hands behind his back. "And since I'm feeling generous today, I won't mention this to your father." He pulled at his goatee worriedly. "And perhaps neither should you."

If I mentioned the beating, I'd have to explain the reason behind it. That could get me into as much trouble as Uncle.

But at least while Father was home, Uncle wouldn't hit me. That calmed me, so I had no trouble speaking. "It will be our little secret," I agreed.

The Dragon

QUESTION: What was your father like?

POP: I didn't know him too good. He'd been in America most of my life.

Uncle Jing insisted on escorting me and Sister home. There were only a half dozen houses in our little village. Plaster had fallen from the outer walls, leaving patches on each house like the markings on dogs. The dark green tiled roofs looked like old straw hats that were coming apart.

To our left was the village pond, which stretched the length of the village. Its muddy surface reflected the gray sky. But when Uncle Fong's pig lapped at the edge, ripples spread outward so that the image wavered and then dissolved.

Beyond the pond, fields spread all the way to a stream

that marked the village's boundary. The earth lay wet and black from the winter rains. Various winter vegetables shoved different leafy tops upward. The land looked like a dark quilt with tufts of green threads dotting the surface.

I liked the fields best when we flooded them and planted rice. I snuck over to my family's fields every chance I got. I loved to watch the crops grow and ripen until the land was covered by a living green fur. Then, when the water was drained away, the fur turned a beautiful gold. And when the wind blew, it was like a giant hand stroking a lion.

To our right was a small hill, and beyond it another sleepy village. In fact, in whatever direction I looked, I could see small villages identical to ours.

The ground between the village and the pond was used for threshing the rice plants. Little bits of straw and chaff clung to Uncle's scholarly robes. He couldn't escape farming no matter how hard he tried.

Up ahead, I could hear the clan welcoming Father. Only Yeps lived in our village. When Father and my brother Yuen had come home almost two years ago, they'd given everyone a present. So the clan was eager to see him.

A few months ago, we'd gotten a letter from Father saying he was returning to China. It was unusual for him to come back so soon. Mother said that he normally waited seven or eight years before he returned for another visit. Everyone figured there had to be some important reason to make him leave the Golden Mountain. A lot of guessing had gone on. Not even Mother knew. Some people said he was going to retire and live off all his gold.

I hoped so. Many Guests came back only as bones to be buried in the cemetery. Grandfather had been one of the first Guests of the Golden Mountain but had made it back alive. Father had even been born there, and had spent most of his life in that strange land. The money he sent home made us rich.

That barbarian land lay to the east—beyond the neighboring villages, beyond the ocean, and just beneath the rising sun. Sometimes at dawn, when the sky was all gold, I thought it reflected the sun shining off the golden peak. And Father would be right on top of the Golden Mountain.

"Here's your son," Uncle Jing announced. People made way for us as if I were royalty. There was Uncle Fong, who thought I teased his pig and upset it. (Well, maybe I did sometimes.) Today he just stepped aside and beamed at me. Cousin Sing patted me on the shoulder.

When we went inside the house, I saw Mother. I had never seen her looking happier. She almost seemed to be hopping up and down. My sister-in-law was busy hushing my nephew. I think all the noise had scared him.

Father stood with his hands clasped behind his back. Even though he had been gone for only two years, he already seemed like a stranger again. And he was so ancient—fifty-four years old!

His vest and robe smelled new, but he didn't seem very comfortable wearing them. His collar was too tight, so he kept fingering it. On his head he did not wear a gentleman's cap with a button on top. Instead, he had a gray Western hat with a wide brim. It looked as if he had shoved his head through a big plate. When he took off his hat, I saw his thick hair. It seemed as hard to tame as mine.

Father frowned at my nephew. The crying was annoying him. Sister-in-Law tried even harder to quiet her child.

Nervously, Mother nudged me. "Don't just stare. Greet your father properly. Or he'll think you're simple."

But the welcome died on my tongue. How could I talk to an important man like him? I felt like such an ant in his giant shadow.

Mother poked me. "You're always talking. What's wrong with you?"

Father smiled. "Do you remember me, boy?"

I didn't really, but I did not want to hurt his feelings, so I lied: "Y-y-yes." In my nervousness, my tongue again began to trip. I felt my cheeks turning red as I started to bow. But when I tried to clasp my hands in front of me,

I had trouble bending the fingers of my left hand. It hurt to curl them.

Father's eyebrows drew together slightly. Had he noticed?

Hastily, I lowered my head. When I straightened, I tried to think of something polite to say. "Great and respected Father," I said formally, "h-h-how was your trip?" It took such an effort to get the sentence out. Father's forehead wrinkled, as if he were having trouble understanding me.

"You're still stammering?" he sighed. "I told you to stop."

Mother smiled apologetically. "I don't know what's wrong with the boy today. He's been doing much better."

Father looked at my injured hand, and then at Uncle Jing. I started to panic. Had Father figured out that I had been bad? "Has my son been very much trouble, Uncle?" he asked Uncle Jing sharply.

Despite Uncle's promise not to tell on me, I held my breath. I was relieved when he simply shook his head. "He's the smartest boy in the school. You should be proud of him. He really does so well when he recites a lesson." That was because I practiced until my speech was flawless. It was hard sometimes to speak smoothly without practice.

Father studied us both thoughtfully. However, he just said to Uncle, "If he's improved, it's because of your teaching. We're grateful for everything you've done."

I wanted to say, *My sour old teacher doesn't deserve any thanks.* But even if I could have trusted my tongue, I knew better.

Uncle Jing attempted a smile. However, he just looked as if he were going to bite someone. This was a special occasion, so he used formal Chinese: "He honors his family."

Father spoke just as formally. "It's we who are honored." Then he waved his hand toward a basket. "I want to give you a small token of our gratitude. I hope you'll come by the day after tomorrow so I can present it."

The rest of the clan was standing outside, in the street. He turned to address them now through the doorway. "Please, all of you come."

Smiling, my uncles, aunts, and cousins accepted eagerly. The recent New Year's celebrations had used up everyone's money. Normally, all the families would have had to skimp on meals afterward. Now they could look forward to a banquet.

There was more polite talk with everyone. Then Sister closed the door. Finally our family was alone.

Father opened the big basket. "But my family doesn't have to wait for two days."

For Mother there was a silver-backed American hand mirror, together with a matching comb and brush. For Sister there were embroidered slippers. "I wasn't sure how big you'd gotten," Father confessed. The slippers were so big, they flopped on her feet when she tried to walk.

Even so, she was squirming with happiness. "I'll stuff paper into the toes," she said.

There was a present for my sister-in-law too, from my brother Yuen. He had stayed in America. And there was also an American toy for my nephew.

Then Father took a small, narrow wooden box from the basket. It had a clever metal catch with a ring. He put his finger into the ring. When he opened the lock, the lid lifted at the same time. "Come here," he said.

My left hand still hurt, so I had trouble taking hold of the box. Mother drew in a sharp breath. She'd figured out I must have used the wrong hand at school.

I cringed, waiting for her to scold me. Father, though, cut her off. He supported the bottom of the box. "Let me hold it for you."

I used my right hand to open and close the lid. I'd never had such a fine thing. When my older sister elbowed me, I remembered to thank Father. I concentrated hard and spoke slowly and carefully, as I had learned to do: "I'll put all my treasures in it." I felt like sighing with relief because I had gotten the sentence out right.

Father smiled in approval. "And take them with you to the Golden Mountain."

Sister stopped in the middle of a step. My mother nearly

dropped the mirror. "He's only ten,"* Mother objected. "We've always waited until the boys were older before they went away."

Father shut the lid of the basket. "He should learn about his other country before . . . before he gets set in his ways."

"He's Chinese," Mother argued. "He was born here."

"He's an American too," Father insisted. "I was born in America. That makes him a citizen." He tapped his wrist. "America's in my bones."

She smiled sadly. "But your son's bones were made in China."

"He has my blood, though," Father insisted proudly. "That makes him American."

Still Mother tried to protest: "It's too soon."

I stood there, scared and miserable. I wasn't ready. I was too young.

Father shook his head sternly. "I've made up my mind. That's the end of the matter."

And Mother fell silent.

* *Nine years by American reckoning. Chinese count the nine months in the womb as a year.*

Scattered in the Wind

QUESTION: Did you want to go to America?

POP: Sure. I didn't have a choice. My father said I had to go. So I went.

I had always known I would have to leave home.

Our village's land was so poor that men in my clan always had to work elsewhere. My grandfather had been one of the first to cross the ocean to the Golden Mountain. Others went to different countries. For generations my clan had been like rice chaff, scattered in the wind all over the world.

Life was supposed to get better after we drove the Manchus out of China eleven years ago. Father had even returned from America to be with us for the happy times.

However, things had only gotten worse. Powerful

generals had set up their own little kingdoms. Then they began to fight one another. Mother prayed every night that the soldiers would stay far away.

Even in the most peaceful of times, life could be hard, with droughts, floods, insects, and plagues. But law and order had disappeared all over China, and that added to our woes. When rival armies weren't invading our district, bandits raided, like locusts that stripped the land bare. People everywhere were starving. So Father returned to America. Until then, Father had been able to support the whole family back in China all by himself. But times became so bad that his money wasn't enough anymore.

One of my older brothers, Yuen, had left to join him in America. Even though the money then doubled, it still wasn't enough. And after I was born, the family had to feed me as well.

My older brother Jong, who was seven years older than me, said I had been an accident. Four of my older brothers were already grown men at the time I was born. No one had expected a seventh child in the family.

Jong said I was so noisy that I drove our other three brothers away. Two went to an area called British Malaya, and another to a country called Mexico.

For a long time, I had believed their leaving was my fault. Since I didn't remember them, I didn't even know what they looked like. So I always felt guilty when my brothers' letters arrived, with their exotic, pretty stamps.

When I was seven, Father held the biggest wedding anyone could remember. It had been for my older brother Yuen. People even came from the neighboring villages to celebrate. Everyone hung on Father's every word, and when people bowed, they bent deep at the waist.

That made me shy around the stranger who was my father. Even when he asked me about something simple, like my schooling, my tongue stumbled. I started to stutter as I had when I had been small. That made him uncomfortable. I tried and tried to speak clearly, but I just couldn't. By the end of his visit, he had stopped talking to me and concentrated on my brother Jong instead.

But who wouldn't? Jong was funnier, smarter, and stronger than me. Though Jong teased me, he had always defended me against bullies. And he had a way of making everyone laugh, especially Father.

Then, after seven months with us, Father went back to the Golden Mountain with Yuen. They had taken Jong along too.

Before they left, I asked Yuen to send me a nugget from the mountain. He had laughed at me. "There's no gold there anymore. It all got taken away."

I missed Jong when he left with Father and Yuen. In exchange, I got a sister-in-law and a noisy nephew who took over our old bedroom. I had to sleep in the parlor now. It didn't seem like a fair swap.

"And how is Jong?" Sister asked.

"Later," Father said hastily. "We have to get a banquet ready for the whole clan."

Mother gave him an odd look. "What happened?"

Father looked around the room as if he wished he could leave. Finally he muttered, "He ran away."

Mother grew pale. "Where?"

Father raised his hands helplessly. "I heard he's working in a railroad crew somewhere, but we can't be sure."

"He's only a boy still. You said you would take care of him." Mother ran into their bedroom. Father followed. Though I couldn't hear, they seemed to be arguing about something.

Sister touched my shoulder. "Come on. We'd better get ready."

Numb inside, I obeyed, working with her and Sister-in-Law. But I moved around like a rod puppet.

When Mother came out later, her eyes were red and puffy. She looked as if she had been crying.

Because I was so scared, I had practiced what I wanted to say over and over, until I could speak it automatically. "I don't want to go," I said to Mother.

She straightened and took a deep breath. Then she went

to a cabinet and, with difficulty, lifted an old, battered suitcase from it. When she opened the suitcase, I saw why it was so heavy. It was full of Chinese paper money. "See this? It's almost worthless. It will take all this currency to buy just one box of matches."

Then she pulled out a cabinet drawer. From it she took an American silver trade dollar. She clutched it to her breast like a magic charm. "I won't spend this. It's a souvenir from your father. But if I did, I could buy baskets of matches with just this one coin. American money is just like magic. Remember, there are two kinds of Chinese. There are ones who went overseas and got rich. And then there are the ones who stayed home and got poor."

"Like Dip Shew?" I asked.

"He had his chance," she said, putting the coin away. "But he thought his wealth was safe, so he stayed here. A drought ruined his crops. He had to sell his land and house. Now he works for us."

"It doesn't seem fair," I said.

Mother shut the lid. "It isn't, but that's why your father and brothers have gone. And that's why you have to go too."

I hugged myself. "But why did Jong run away?"

"Jong ran away because he was . . . a bad boy." Her face was so sad, though, that I don't think she believed that. "He wouldn't listen to your father. You have to be better than Jong." She put away the suitcase. "But you mustn't tell anyone. Do you understand?"

"Yes," I said in a small voice.

It wasn't easy being the son of a dragon from a village of dragons. But I swallowed and said, "I'll try."

The next morning Father went north with Dip Shew, heading for the market town. They came back with a whole roast pig. And there were roast ducks that you ate with plum sauce, and buns light as air. However, Father had also wanted teas and spices that the market town did not have. Father complained about that.

"It's not San Francisco," Mother reminded him.

The day after that, I made makeshift tables by laying boards over trestles while Sister and Sister-in-Law cooked. Our house had two kitchens, and since so many people were coming, we used both of them. It was my job to feed straw and wood into the openings at the front of the stoves. I had to keep running from one kitchen to another.

When everything was almost ready, Sister got my special clothes out of a chest.

I put on my blue satin robe and black vest. I set the black cap on my head. Sister fussed over me: "Now you look like a real son of a Guest of the Golden Mountain." She added, "So I want you to sit on that bench until the banquet."

⇌   ⇌   ⇌

When our guests came, they brought their own benches and chairs and extra tables so that everyone could sit and eat. There were a lot of speeches welcoming Father home. There was a lot of feasting.

Then Uncle had me recite one of my lessons. I closed my eyes so I wouldn't see everyone staring. I'd rehearsed the poem a lot over the past two days. It was called "The Wanderer's Homecoming." I didn't make one mistake, and Uncle nodded and said, "Good, good."

Father beamed with satisfaction.

As the clan toasted him, I saw again how everyone in the village treated Father like a lord. He really must be rich in the land of the Golden Mountain. He must own a big store and employ lots of people. He was not just a dragon: he was a dragon king. What could I do for someone that important? Maybe he expected me to help him count his money.

The whole clan was curious. Finally Uncle Jing asked Father about his business in America.

"Good, good," Father said, and quickly changed the topic.

Even in the middle of the toasts in his honor, there were times when Father didn't seem to fit in. When the clan tried to catch him up on the local gossip, he could barely keep from yawning. He only perked up when an uncle told him about a Guest from a nearby village who had built a house there like the ones in San Francisco. "That's a swell idea," he said.

The whole clan laughed. "No one uses the word 'swell' anymore," said one of the relatives.

Even though Father had been home two years ago, a lot of his slang was already outdated. Or sometimes he used words from the dialect of Canton, the capital of the province.* They had slipped into his vocabulary in San Francisco. The village teased him, calling him a city slicker.

Father's smile became thinner and tighter as the afternoon wore on. Though the banquet was in his honor, he looked a little sad and distant. It was as if the celebration weren't for him but for someone else.

He began to seem impatient for it to end. He tugged at his collar more and more. And he squirmed worse than my nephew.

He seemed glad when Mother suggested he should hand out the promised presents. Father gave bars of American soap to everyone. They all sniffed their fragrant gifts. American soap was harder than the soap here. It would last longer. It had a kind of perfume too. There was also a clock for my teacher, shawls for my aunts, cigars for

* Provinces in China were geographical and governmental units— like the states are in America. In China, districts make up each province just as counties make up many states in America.

my uncles, and candy for my cousins. Everyone said this was better than the New Year's celebrations.

We kept my runaway brother Jong a secret from the whole clan.

The next morning, Father excused me from helping to clean up from the banquet. He said it was time to prepare for the test.

"What t-test?" I asked uneasily.

Father scratched his head. "You spoke so well at the welcoming banquet. What's happened to you?"

I was afraid to speak again, so I just shrugged.

Father looked both confused and frustrated. "He's fine when he's calm and has time to think," Mother explained.

"Ah," Father said, and clasped his hands behind his back. Now he looked as uneasy as I felt. I don't think he knew what to do with children.

"Perhaps you might tell him about the Americans' test," Mother suggested.

"Yes, of course." Father cleared his throat. "The Americans are going to ask us a lot of questions about our family and our village."

"Are they that curious about us?" I asked, puzzled.

"No. They don't want Chinese in their country. So when a man goes over to China, they want to make sure it's the same person trying to get back into the Golden

23

Mountain." Father patted his chest. "In your case, they'll want to be certain you're my son."

I was even more confused. "H-how could strangers know so much about us?"

"Each time one of our clan goes to America, they ask questions," Father said. "They've been doing that for years, so they have a lot of information. All your answers have to be right."

I was so shocked, my stutter got worse. "W-hat h-happens if I g-get something wr- . . . wr- . . ."—my ears burned as I fought to finish the sentence—". . . wrong?"

Father hesitated. "Do you remember your older brother Yuen?"

I fought hard to speak clearly. "Yes, I met him when he got married."

"Well, when he first went to America, he made a mistake about our fields. But the Americans know how important land is to us." Father licked his lips as if the memory still scared him. "They figured he wasn't my son. They said he was an impostor who had no right to enter America. He was almost sent home. That's why he made sure to study so he wouldn't get in trouble on his next round trip between China and America." That would have been two years ago, after the wedding.

When Yuen had come back for the wedding, I had thought it funny that he and Jong had gone around looking at the fields and the village. They even memo-rized the number of windows and doors on the walls of each house.

"H-how did Yuen do the second time? And what about J-Jong?" I asked.

"It was hard, but they both got through," Father said. "That's why you have to work as much as they did."

"W-why do Americans m-make it so hard to g-get into their country?" I asked.

"They just do it to Chinese," Father sighed. "They blame us for a lot of their troubles. If we came from any other country, we'd have no problem getting into America."

"That's not f-fair," I said indignantly.

"That's the way it is," Mother said.

"And it's not *all* the Americans," Father added. "There are many kind ones who are my friends. It's the American officials we have to worry about. We have to prove to them who we are."

"B-but y-you said we w-were Americans," I protested. "Sh-shouldn't I learn about America?"

Father laughed sadly. "That's the odd part. To be Americans, we have to show how Chinese we are. But you want to know what's funny? The families of some of those American officials might have been in America fewer years than ours."

Later, Father and I took a walk through the village and the fields. Everywhere, Father was greeted with bows and smiles. In between bowing and smiling himself, Father quizzed me.

"Who lives in that house?" Father asked, pointing at a cousin's home as we passed. When I told him, he wanted to know if they had a rice mill, a device that removed the tough hulls that covered the rice grains.

My tongue stumbled, along with my memory. "I th-think so."

"You can't think," Father said grimly. "You have to *know*. Make even the slightest error and the Americans will kick you out."

The test was sounding harder and harder. "Is that the w-worst that would happen?" It would be bad to waste all that money on the cost of a ticket, but I thought we could afford it.

"Everyone thinks we're wealthy. And I'll admit we're comfortable." Father held up his right hand with the palm flat and facing the ground. "But everything's balanced on a knife blade." He wobbled his hand and let it tilt sideways. "The government, the warlords, the bandits—they all have their hands out for money and more money. And when they aren't stealing from us, they're fighting each other. One battle could destroy our village, as so many others have been destroyed."

"You mean we h-have to g-g- . . . ?" My cheeks reddened at the clumsiness of my tongue, and I took my time before I tried to speak again: "We have to go overseas?"

"Yes, so we can't give the Americans an excuse to turn us away." Father looked scared at the notion. "When the Americans thought Yuen was a liar, they said I must be liar too. They tried to send us both back to China. Fail the test and they'll ship you, me, and him out. And that would be a disaster."

"I'll . . . I'll tr-tr- . . ." My fear made my tongue betray me completely, and I couldn't finish the sentence.

Father clasped his hands behind his back. "You have to control that stammer of yours. It's not enough to know the correct information. It's also *how* you answer. If you stutter during the test, the Americans will think you're hiding something."

Worse and worse. If my memory didn't fail me, I knew my tongue would. And then we'd lose the house and fields and everything else. And then Mother, Sister, my sister-in-law, and my nephew would starve.

And it would all be my fault.

Ching Ming

QUESTION: *What were your grandparents like?*

POP: *They had died a long time before I was born.*

As the days grew into weeks, Father finished discussing
business matters with Mother. By then I knew the village
inside and out and my answers were starting to be
smoother. It was then that Father started to grow bored.
And the more bored he became, the more he complained.

"Can't you do anything about that blasted rooster?"
Father said one morning, yawning. "He crows too loud
and too early."

Mother chuckled. "You're too used to the city. You're
on a farm now."

Then Father got tired of "country food." I thought
Sister and Sister-in-Law's cooking was just fine, but

Father went all the way to Toisan, the district capital, to buy a special type of pepper from Szechuan. A favorite restaurant in San Francisco used it in a spicy chicken that was his favorite dish. He came back disgusted because no one stocked the pepper, even though Toisan was the biggest city in the district.

Finally, one evening he threw up his hands. "I'm fed up with this place. There's nothing to do here. In San Francisco I can see a different opera every night," he complained.

"Sometimes I think you're more San Franciscan than Chinese," Mother teased gently. "You act more like a Guest of China than of America."

"I can't help it if I was born there," Father replied, shrugging. "When you live in a place for the first thirteen years of your life, you get used to certain things."

Mother sighed. "How can you love a place where the Americans make it so hard for you?"

Father looked away. "China wasn't any easier. People are nice to me now because they think I'm rich. But when my parents first brought me back here, all the other boys made fun of me behind my back. No matter how hard I tried, China never felt like home."

Mother folded her hands in front of her and looked at him sadly. "I could see how unhappy you were the first year we were married. At first I thought it was me. Then I realized it was living in China."

"It's what I am," Father said, just as sadly.

I stared up at him, this strange man who was my father. His life here didn't fit him any better than his robe did.

During the Ching Ming, Father announced that he and I would visit my grandparents together.

The Ching Ming was a spring festival when people went to their family graves and cleaned them. They also offered food and drink to the departed.

Father carried a basket of food as we left the house. Farmers were flooding the fields, and muddy water was slowly hiding the dirt. Soon Dip Shew would transplant the seedlings of the first rice crop into my family's land.

This was my favorite time of year. I usually helped Dip Shew. The mud would ooze between my toes as I stuck the seedlings into it. The water was like a mirror. I could see my reflection, and those of the clouds and the village. This was where I belonged.

I wished Father would leave me here to farm with Dip Shew.

It was an hour's walk to my grandparents' graves to the north. I had never met them. They had died long before I was born.

I was in my good clothes, so I had to walk on the path between the fields.

As we walked, Father went on quizzing me about the village. I tried my best to answer without stuttering.

It wasn't long before Father wiped the dust from his forehead. "What a primitive country," he muttered. "In San Francisco, we could ride cable cars anywhere we wanted to go. You'll like it there."

Was there anything he liked about China? I couldn't ask him, though, without being rude.

Eventually we reached the cemetery. There were no markers on the hill; there were only small mounds of dirt. Last year, Mother had brought me and Dip Shew to clean them, but the summer rains had brought the weeds back so that everything was now covered in green fuzz.

People were scattered around the slope, tending to their relatives. Some were laughing. Some were even singing. They too had baskets of food and drink to share with their dead.

I followed Father up the hillside. He moved confidently toward one mound.

I stopped with him. My grandparents had both died in China and lay together now.

Father bowed solemnly, bending at the waist once, twice, three times.

I copied Father.

Then Father bent over to clean the graves. However, I remembered what Dip Shew had done. I squatted down the way he did in our rice fields. So it wasn't so hard on the back.

Father weeded very slowly and clumsily. He might wear fancy robes and everyone might treat him like a lord, but he was terrible at weeding. Dip Shew had stripped the mound for us in a wink of an eye. Whatever Father had learned when he lived in China, it hadn't been farming.

Father also pulled the weeds up by their stems. They broke with crisp snaps, leaving their roots. However, I tried to yank up the roots as well. Dip Shew had explained that this way, the weeds would not overrun the mound in a thick mat and they would be easier to remove the next year.

When the grave was clear, Father straightened up and rubbed his back. "Are you all r-r-right?" I asked.

He looked as if he was about to remind me not to stutter. But when I hung my head, he just cleared his throat. "I've got just a bit of an ache. What about you?"

Because I had copied Dip Shew, my back felt fine, though my legs hurt. I didn't trust my tongue not to annoy Father, so I just shook my head.

He studied his dirty fingers. "I'm a city boy. I'm just not used to this."

I felt sorry for him. He couldn't help it if he was born in America. He wasn't used to farming. Or roosters. Or farm cooking. Or anything to do with the country. It was just as he said: China wasn't his home.

I took my time before speaking. "You're an important man."

He smiled, pleased because I had spoken clearly. "Time to bring out the meal," he said, dusting off his hands.

Sitting down for a picnic, we gave the best to my grandparents. Father and I would eat the rest.

Sister had packed buns with lots of meat, and I wolfed one of them down. Some of the other families had also sat down to eat, but their meals were simple and meager.

As he munched away, Father said, "We owe everything to your grandfather. If you think things are bad in China now, they were even worse back then. But your grandfather freed us from all of that. Without him, we would have starved. He was a brave man. He went over to China when the voyage was difficult. On some boats, one out of every three men died."

That made me feel even smaller. My grandfather had saved my family. And then there were my father and my brothers. How could I ever match them?

"Even now, he and your grandmother watch over us," Father said. "We buried them in a place that collects a lot of good energy, ch'i, and they send it on to us." The universe was filled with that invisible ch'i, and it was possible to channel it.

As we were eating, a family near us scurried over and thriftily picked up the weeds we had discarded. Fuel for kitchen stoves was costly. They would save our unwanted plants for cooking. They picked up even the small bits. Father didn't care, though.

As I watched them gather up our trash, I felt sorry for them. But I also felt proud. Because of my grandparents and my father and my brothers, we weren't like them. We were Guests of the Golden Mountain. And that made us different.

I told myself that it was time for me to do my share so we wouldn't ever be like the poor family scrambling for our throwaway weeds. I'd remember everything about our village. And I would describe it clearly to the Americans.

Father looked down the hill, toward the road. "It's time to go home."

He wasn't looking back toward our village, though. Instead, he was looking east, toward the sea and the Land of the Golden Mountain.

His home.

But not mine.

Farewell to the Village

QUESTION: Were you sad when you left your village?

POP: Maybe a little . . . well, maybe a lot.

Even though Father was more than willing to leave, he made me rehearse my answers for months, until I could speak them more or less clearly. Finally he said that I was as ready as I ever would be.

On my last morning in the village, it was already warm and muggy. It would be the kind of summer day to play in the pond.

Soon it would be time for the harvest. That was always a happy, exciting time. Dip Shew would bend over in the drained fields. Then his sickle would slice through the rice stalks with a crisp, crunching sound. He would straighten up and move on to the next set of stalks. He sang while he did that. It was like a dance.

And I would miss it.

Don't think about that, I told myself.

From one of the kitchens, I heard Sister starting the fire. I knew her routine by heart. First she would heat gruel made from yesterday's leftover rice. It was good, plain food, but she had a way of making it tasty with onions and preserved eggs. I thought I could also smell pork. Maybe there would be some slices of that as a special treat.

This was my last morning at home. I looked around the parlor one final time. Silently I said a prayer to our ancestors in the shrine in the loft overhead. Then I closed my eyes and tried to dream again. Overhead, the summer rains drummed on the roof.

A finger prodded my shoulder. "Wake up, sleepy," Sister said. I smelled sugarcane syrup on her fingertips.

Opening my eyes, I saw her holding a piece of sugarcane. It was my favorite treat.

Even as my mouth watered, I felt an ache inside. Would I ever see her again?

"Well, take it," she said, thrusting it at me. "I haven't got all day." But she was grinning.

"Thank you." I meant to eat it slowly and savor every bite. However, it tasted too good. I wolfed it down greedily. Then I licked the lovely sweetness from my fingers.

"So you liked it a little bit." She laughed as she tapped my head. "Now get dressed."

She had already laid out my clothes for the trip.

I picked up the shirt. The seams were stiff from a recent ironing. Sister lingered in the doorway to the main kitchen. "Everyone who sees you will say you come from a family that does things right," she said. Suddenly the corners of her mouth drooped and tears started to roll down her cheeks. Turning, she hurried into one of the kitchens. I knew she would miss me even if she wouldn't admit it. I'd miss her too. Maybe most of all.

Mother walked briskly into the room. She nodded approvingly when she saw that I was already dressed. She helped me roll up the bedding. I would take that with me.

Usually it was my chore to take apart my bed. Today, though, she did it with me. Together we lifted the bedding off the planks and put away the trusses. This would be the last time I would do this for a long while. Perhaps for forever.

She stared at me. Her lip trembled. But she didn't say anything. That was never her way. She showed her love by working hard for everyone.

I went into the kitchen where Sister was cooking. She was frying fresh crullers in the wok. She was still crying. A tear sizzled in the hot oil. "It's all this smoke," she said self-consciously, and waved a hand.

The smoke drifted around the windowless room, pressing up against the skylight. Water rippled across the glass.

I squatted before the opening at the front of the stove. Picking up a handful of grass and twigs, I tossed them onto the fire. *After I leave, who will tend the flames for her?* I wondered. My nephew was still too small.

Then I got plates and cups and bowls, soup spoons and chopsticks, and brought them into the parlor. As I was setting the table, Father and Mother sat upon a bench, discussing last-minute things. He was still in his fancy robe.

I ate quickly and silently while the grown-ups talked. Then Dip Shew knocked on the main door. Because of the heavy rains, Father had hired a cart. "The cart's here," he said.

"It's time," Father said, laying his chopsticks over the mouth of the bowl. This was a signal to everyone that he was done.

When he got up, I rose too, but my legs felt wobbly. Mother and Sister rushed to the main door.

Dip Shew shouldered my rolled-up bedding as well as Father's, and carried it out to the cart. He took out the suitcase with our clothes next.

I picked up the box with my treasures. It had been hard, choosing them for the trip. I could hear them rattling in the box.

I didn't want to go. It was hard to follow Father as he made his way toward the large door.

As we approached, Sister opened it. Then both Mother and Sister bowed. My sister-in-law also lowered her head. She was holding my nephew, and she leaned him forward in a kind of bow. One of these days, it would be his turn to leave too.

They were all trying to smile, but they looked as if they were going to cry.

As I crossed the threshold, the departure hit me suddenly. Would I ever see home again? Would I ever see my mother and sister? Or my sister-in-law and nephew?

I sniffed, trying to hold back my tears.

"Be a good boy, now," Mother whispered. "Don't give your father any trouble."

I was glad Father had his back to me. I wiped my eyes hastily on my sleeve.

Dip Shew was covering our things, now on the back of the cart, with an oiled cloth. He called cheerfully, "Send me some gold nuggets from the Mountain, all right?"

My cousins and uncles were all outside. They told me to listen to Father. By the village well, my aunts were hauling up water. They wished us good luck. There was a sign over the school. THE FAMILY IS EVERYTHING. It was one last lesson from Uncle Jing.

As the cart rolled south along the path, the wind blew

and raindrops hit my face. The rice fields on either side of us had been drained. The first rice crop was ripening. The heads were bent, heavy with grain. I hoped the rain wouldn't spoil the crops. It was one more reason to work in America.

Boys were walking along dike paths, coming from neighboring villages to our school. They dragged their feet, digging their heels into the damp earth. Soon they would be with Uncle and his bamboo rod.

They halted when they saw me. I raised a hand to them. They only stared.

That upset me so much that I turned to Father. "W-what's wrong? Th-they act like I'm a g-g-ghost."

As I knew it would, my stammer made him frown, but he explained: "It's not that. You're not one of them anymore. You're now a Guest of the Golden Mountain. That makes you a man."

I tried to sit up as straight and proud as one.

But inside, I didn't feel that way at all.

Hong Kong

QUESTION: *What did you think of Hong Kong?*

POP: *I never saw anything like it before. I was just this little hick from the countryside.*

I huddled under the umbrella as the rain rattled against the oiled paper. I'd been on this road once before, when I'd gone to town. I'd had a photograph taken to send to Father. Up until then, I had always been in sight of my home. Now I was going to go far beyond that.

The heavy rain hid the passing villages behind a silvery curtain. Houses seemed like paper cutouts.

Despite the weather, Father began to quiz me again. "If you can do it under the worst conditions, you can do it anywhere," he said.

I did my best to answer. But sometimes the wind

drove the rain into my face and I spluttered.

A sudden gust twisted my umbrella inside out and snapped a quarter of the ribs. Father had managed to save his own. He gave it to me now.

I tried to share it, but I could only cover half of him. Water poured off his hat brim on his exposed side. Even then, he kept questioning me.

The cart let us off at the railroad station. The rain crashed down even harder as we boarded the train. It was as if the sky wanted to keep me here. But the locomotive was too powerful. This was my first train ride. As the engine chugged along, I pressed my nose excitedly against the window, trying to see the landscape. There was so much water splashing against the glass that everything was blurred. Father said it was a good thing, because there were bandits all around. They wouldn't be able to rob the train.

Every now and then, I glimpsed burned houses, even villages, through the silvery curtain. Was it a feuding clan or bandits or soldiers who had set them on fire? But seeing the destruction made me realize Mother was right. We needed more American silver dollars. They would protect the family like a magic charm. With them we could bribe our enemies. Or we could rebuild.

If I passed my test.

If I spoke clearly.

That thought made me so scared that I started to stutter

again while I rehearsed my answers. Father looked anxious. I wondered if he was already sorry he had taken me along.

We switched trains in Toisan. Like green snakes seeking a meal, tree-covered mountain ranges wriggled toward the city from several angles. To the northwest, a tall pagoda rose like a fang from the highest peak of one range.

The drenched houses were pressed together like ducks about to be eaten. I'd never seen so many tall houses. Some were two or even three stories high. But Father said I should wait until I saw San Francisco.

After riding for a while, we changed trains again, getting off at another city. There we boarded a steamer. I'd had my first train rides. Now it was my first time on a boat. I wanted to go out on deck, but it was too wet. Father said I would soon get my fill of ships.

When the boat got within sight of Hong Kong, I couldn't see how any city could be bigger. Though there were farms around its borders, buildings covered the hills. Even on flat land, they would have towered over the hills near our village. Some of Hong Kong's structures looked as big as mountains. And there were so many of them! It looked as if a flock of stone and wooden ducks had settled on the slopes.

Father saw my wide eyes and understood what I was thinking. "Hong Kong's nothing, boy," he boasted. "In San Francisco, the buildings are even taller." Father seemed to think everything was bigger and better in San Francisco.

And all the people! I didn't know there were that many people in the world. They jammed the wet streets. It was late afternoon. The rain had stopped, so pedestrians had put away their umbrellas. Some of the men sweated in robes and vests. Black Chinese caps fit their skulls tightly.

However, many of the townsmen wore Western-style felt hats on their heads, as Father had when he'd first come home. Some of them wore straw hats. The Western brims stuck out.

I had no trouble sticking close to Father, because he couldn't have rushed if he wanted to. It was just too crowded.

"Grab my vest, boy," he said. His arms were full, since he was carrying our bedding and the suitcase.

I clung to his clothing with one hand. With the other I held on to my box tightly. I bumped into Father's back when he stopped suddenly before a tall building. The sign said it was some kind of company. As on many other signs, there were words in Chinese, but the sign also had the strange strokes of English words.

We entered the building and staggered up the crowded stairs. It was a very busy place.

Panting, Father spoke to a clerk at a desk. "You're in luck," the man said. "There's a ship leaving for America in five days."

Father nodded at me. "I'll need passage for two."

The clerk stared at me in surprise. "He looks awfully young."

"He's very smart," Father insisted. "He'll pass the tests."

"You're asking for trouble," the clerk said, but he handed Father some papers.

When Father finished his business, he picked up our things and clumped up the next flight of stairs. There didn't seem to be any end to them. This building was as high as the hill behind our village. How could they build something so tall? With each step I was afraid it would fall. On the fourth floor, we finally stopped and entered a large room. The kitchen next to it was dark.

There were a dozen men in the room. They had spread their bedding on the floor. Next to them were their suitcases. It looked as if they were all Guests going back to America.

One of the men in the room greeted Father. "Hey, Lung Gon," he called. "You can take these spots right over here." He was a man in his late forties. "Who's your shadow?" he asked, pointing at me.

Father started to spread out our bedding on the floor next to the man. "Ah Lee, I want you to meet my youngest. He's going to help me in America."

A man with a big wart on his neck laughed harshly. "He's too young. The Americans will eat him up alive."

Ah Lee waved his hand at Wart Man. "Don't pay any

attention to him. He always expects the worst."

"You'll be fine," Father assured me. He couldn't wait to shed his lovely robe and vest. Gone was the rich, important lord of the village. In his place stood a true Guest of the Golden Mountain in a Western-style suit. I stared because it was the first time I'd seen Father dressed that way. "This calls for a celebration," he said.

"What do you have to be so cheerful about?" Wart Man demanded, rolling onto his side to stare at us. "We're leaving home for that awful place."

"The Golden Mountain's our home," Ah Lee explained. "He was born there, just like me."

Wart Man knocked at the side of his head. "Native-born have no brains."

Father didn't let Wart Man's rudeness spoil his own good mood. Instead, he nodded to Ah Lee. "Can I treat you to dinner?"

Ah Lee liked to laugh. "Are you as tired of country cooking as I am?"

Father grinned sheepishly. "I miss my favorites. We can go to the Golden Dragon. It's next to the tailor's."

I was tired and being in a strange place upset me, so I slipped back into my old habits. "But it's so l-l-late," I said. Through the window, I could see the sun setting.

Father smiled. "This is Hong Kong, not our boring little village. It never sleeps." He held up his index finger.

"And what have I been telling you?"

I spoke carefully. "Don't . . ."—I caught my tongue as it began to trip—"stutter."

With a satisfied smile, Father picked up the robe and vest and led Ah Lee and me outside. The street was even more crowded than before. Only a few men were dressed in as completely modern a fashion as Father.

Eagerly, Father made his way through the maze of streets, more at home in the city than he had ever been in the village. The tailor shop was still open. I'd never seen so much cloth. Just beyond it, the restaurant was bright with light.

"I'll get a table," Ah Lee said, disappearing inside.

Within his shop, the tailor was having dinner. He put down his chopsticks when we entered. "Back so soon?" he asked. "You Guests are all the same. As soon as you feel some country mud between your toes, you want to leave."

Father set down the robe and vest. "I'm returning the rental," he said. He looked glad to be rid of them.

I looked at Father in surprise. I had thought the fancy clothes were his own. After all, wasn't he a rich man?

The tailor inspected the robe and vest for damage. Satisfied, he put them away. On the shelves of the wardrobe, I saw dozens of folded-up robes and vests for rent. They were all sizes and colors. "You really looked good in this outfit. You ought to buy it."

Father rubbed his neck as if remembering how tight

the robe's collar was. "I don't wear that stuff on the Golden Mountain. But you can make an American suit for my son."

My dark cotton shirt and pants didn't seem strange to me. It's what all the boys wore at home. It's what the boys in Hong Kong wore too.

I wanted to ask what was wrong with my clothes, so I pointed to my shirt and raised a puzzled eyebrow.

Father shrugged. "You look fine for China, but not America."

I couldn't help saying to myself, *Is he ashamed of me?*

In the meantime, the tailor had already taken out a basket. Inside were pictures clipped from Western magazines. I couldn't read the words, because they were in English. Father went through the pictures. Finally he picked one up and held it next to me. "Yes, this one."

I stared. "You're getting ch-cheated. The pants are too short."

"It's what all modern young gentlemen wear," the tailor wheedled. "The Westerners* call them knickerbockers."

"Learn that word," my father instructed me. He sounded like Uncle Jing at that moment. I repeated the syllables slowly, for they felt strange to my tongue.

As I practiced saying the word, the tailor took out a

---

* *The term "Westerners" is a polite way to refer to Caucasians in Chinese.*

cloth tape measure. Then he measured and measured me.

When he was finally finished, we went next door, to the restaurant. There were big black shiny round tables everywhere. And almost every chair was filled. I'd never eaten among so many strangers before. They talked so loud too. Their voices were like the roaring of a river.

Suddenly I felt shy. I pressed close to Father.

Ah Lee waved us over to a big table. It could have sat ten people rather than three. "I had to fight off three different groups for this table," Ah Lee boasted.

When Father finished ordering from a waiter, I understood the reason. It wasn't the chairs we needed, it was the table itself.

There was duck smoked in tea leaves, and huge prawns with nuts in a honey sauce, and beef and lamb, and some fish I didn't recognize—enough food for an emperor. I didn't know there were so many ways to cook food. The dishes covered the broad table.

As Father picked up a slice of beef from a plate, he sighed. "It was nice to be home at first. But the food is always the same."

"San Francisco has spoiled my taste buds too," Ah Lee agreed as he raised his cup of tea. "To the Golden Mountain," he toasted. "It's a place of tears, but it's never boring."

Father lifted his own cup. "To the Golden Mountain

and its variety—from food to people."

I ate and ate. I lost count of the dishes, each was so delicious. When I was stuffed, I felt calm enough to ask a question. "You eat like this all the time?" I asked Father. It was a little victory to speak clearly.

"Well, not all the time, but as often as I can," Father admitted.

Father must be even richer than I thought.

"I think your stays in China get shorter and shorter," Ah Lee said.

Father shrugged. "You know how it is."

Ah Lee nodded sympathetically. "I always feel like a stranger here too."

I rehearsed my protest before I uttered it. "But you're Chinese," I said, echoing Mother.

"We belong to both countries," Father insisted, waving a hand at Ah Lee. "So that makes us something new."

His friend lifted one shoulder. "But is it good to be so different? Sometimes I think you and I are changelings. When we were born there, some American souls got lost and wandered into the wrong babies."

"Right now, the only thing inside me is plenty of duck." Father patted his satisfied stomach.

That night, when I closed my eyes, I tried to pretend I was home again. But it was just too noisy. At home, the only sounds at night were the frogs and the insects. In the city, voices and carts and everything else were still merging into a steady roar.

I couldn't sleep at all. Father, though, had started snoring right away, despite the noisy crowds outside. He was used to the din of the city, not the quiet of our village.

I remembered again how everything in the village had bothered Father. He might be an important man, but he really didn't fit into our clan. From what he had told Mother, he never had.

He reminded me of a man from an old fairy tale. This man had watched two sages play a game of chess. When he finally left the game, he found that years had passed in the outside world. And everything had changed in his village. He stuck out like a flagpole.

So did Father when he left the Golden Mountain to go back to our village.

Would I stick out just as much when I returned home? Would I even make it to America?

The New Skin

QUESTION: *Were you nervous about America?*

POP: *The village was all I knew up until then. So it was going to be a big change.*

The next day, Father took me to a store. It was filled with Western shoes made of leather. When I tried on a pair, they felt heavy and stiff compared to my cloth ones. When I tried to walk in them, I clopped around. "They make me feel like a water buffalo," I complained. To my relief, I wasn't stuttering. Maybe that was because I was getting used to being with Father.

Father was determined to make me into an American boy. "You'll get used to them," he said, and pointed to his own leather shoes.

Father bought me stockings too, and then took me to another store to buy a hat. He had me try on a flat cap with a visor. As I was looking at myself in a mirror, I saw my first Westerners. They were shopping too.

"Are they Americans?" I whispered to Father.

One of them, a man, understood what I'd said. He laughed and said in Chinese, "No, we're British. Thank Heaven."

Once we were outside, I wanted to switch back to my old shoes, but Father wouldn't let me. "You have to break them in."

They cramped my feet, though. I thought it would be the other way around: the shoes would shape my feet into something strange.

There was so much to see and do that I soon forgot about the tight, ugly shoes. We climbed up steep streets to a high peak. Mist covered the water, but I could just about make out another city across the way. The buildings were patches of pink. "Is that Hong Kong too?"

"No, it's Macao," Father said. "The Portuguese own it."

In my Western shoes, I clopped all over Hong Kong with Father. That hazy day and the next two, I hardly ever stuttered, so he rarely scolded me.

Finally my new clothes were ready. There was a suit and a vest of some gray material. They looked so funny.

I took off my loose black cotton clothes. When I pulled on the pants, I frowned. They bunched up at the knees and left my calves bare except for my stockings.

Cautiously, I put on the rest of the Western suit. The coat was cut close to my body. The whole suit would fit tight even in the dry season, but in the humid weather now, it stuck to me like a new skin. And the cloth was so heavy! I felt as if I were in an oven. Even my satin robe and vest were more comfortable.

I tugged and pulled at the material. "This stuff makes me feel all hot," I grumbled. At least I wasn't stuttering.

Father's forehead wrinkled, as if I were a puzzle. "When you get to San Francisco, you'll be glad it does. It's foggy there."

"It's itchy too," I said, wriggling my shoulders and then trying to tug the pants lower to cover my calves. "People can see part of my legs."

The tailor cajoled me. "This is the best suit for America," he said.

My hands found the knickerbockers' pockets and slid inside them. "But I don't want to be an American."

"Well, then you don't have to slouch like one." Father tapped me on the shoulder. "Straighten up and take your hands out of your pockets."

I slipped my hands free of my knickerbockers resentfully. "I feel like a clown."

Father looked just like I probably did when I was trying to figure out what to say and how to say it.

"That's what you're going to wear," he finally muttered. "You don't need these old clothes anymore. We'll send them back home now for your nephew to have when he's old enough."

Father had made me leave my special clothes behind. My nephew would get them, along with my old school desk. And my toys. And my whole life.

"He gets everything of mine," I complained.

"He gets the past," Father explained. "You get the future."

As the tailor picked up my dark cotton shirt and pants, I felt like a snake that had shed its skin. Except that for me, my old skin had been loose and comfortable. This new skin was choking me.

Father was trying to make me into a Guest, just like himself.

Resentfully, I followed Father out of the shop. When he wasn't looking, I stuck my hands back in my pockets and let my shoulders sag. If I had to dress like an American boy, I'd slouch like one too.

Though we could have taken meals in the building where we were staying, Father preferred to eat out. We ate at several different restaurants during our stay. At first, eating all the different food dishes was fun. But soon I missed Mother's cooking, just as I missed her hugs.

However, on our last day in Hong Kong, Father bought vegetables and meat from various stalls. The cook in the kitchen of the building let us have some room at the stove and allowed us to use his utensils.

Ah Lee had also bought some food. Father and he decided to combine everything for another banquet.

Father began to slice a piece of beef as efficiently as Sister. I stared at him. "I didn't know you could cook."

Ah Lee laughed. "That's all your father does on the Golden Mountain."

"It's not all," Father sniffed.

"You own a restaurant?" I asked.

"I did a long time ago, but it was in a place called New Mexico. It was way too hot." Father pantomimed wiping his forehead.

"What do you do now?" I asked curiously.

Ah Lee turned to Father in surprise. "You haven't told him you're a *houseboy*?"

Father snapped at Ah Lee: "I was waiting for the right time."

"When? When you got back into the Americans' kitchen?" Ah Lee demanded.

Father ignored Ah Lee and looked at me. "I work for the Dugans, a brother and a sister. Mr. Dugan is an important man. He's a chemist. That's another name for a kind of herbalist who makes medicines. On Fridays he buys enchiladas, so I don't even have to cook that day. And his sister is very sweet. You'll like them. And they're both looking forward to meeting you."

I had figured Father was a rich, important man. "You cook for them?"

"And wash and clean," Father said, blushing. "I keep house for them."

Puzzled, I wrinkled my forehead. My important father, dusting? The clan would have laughed at the notion. "Don't you have a big desk and an office?"

"No," Father said. "Just a stove and a broom."

"But we're so rich," I protested. "How can you be a servant?"

Father sighed. "We're rich compared to our neighbors. But that's because the American money I earn is worth so much more in China. It's honest work. There's nothing to be ashamed of."

I stood there, stunned. He'd gone from being a dragon king to an American servant. No wonder he hadn't told the clan what he did. How could I trust him now?

"You won't be a prince over there," Ah Lee warned me. "You'll be the son of a servant."

"You'll help me with some of the chores, but you'll have to go to school too," Father explained. "Mr. Dugan feels very strongly about that."

The news about school was an even worse shock.

"M-more Chinese lessons?" I stuttered. Would my Chinese teachers be like Uncle Jing?

"Well, you'll be in an American school. You'll have to learn English," Father said.

"B-but why?" I whined.

Father clicked his tongue in exasperation. "Because it's what they speak over there. But don't worry. We won't neglect your Chinese. There's a school for that in the evening too."

This was even more horrible. Double the schoolwork! I'd rather dig ditches. I bit my lip. I remembered what Mother had said when she had shown me the American silver dollar. "The only r-reason we go over there is to make m-money. How c-can I do that w-when I'm in t-two schools?" I was almost in tears. "Why can't I w-wait till l-later, when I'm done with school?"

Father seemed to have more thoughts in his head than words. Frustrated, he chopped at a melon. "You're going because . . . because I say so. That should be enough for a good boy." Father's knife began to slice a piece of melon into slivers. The knife went click-click-click against the chopping board.

I felt like he was cutting me up too.

Ah Lee could see how miserable I was. "Your father—" he began.

Father glared at his friend. "Shut up! You leave this to me."

Ah Lee turned away heavily. "Have it your way, but you're making the same mistake all over again."

"W-what mistake?" I demanded.

"Never mind," Father said.

"The same mistake all over again," Ah Lee repeated, looking worried.

The Ship

QUESTION: *What ship did you take?*

POP: *The S.S.* China. *It was a hot day when we got on it, and it was even hotter inside.*

June 27, 1922

The next day, I wouldn't speak to Father. At first he tried to get me to talk. However, I didn't trust him anymore. He'd lied about his job. Worse, he hadn't told me about the double schooling. I had to obey him, even if he was being mean. But I didn't have to chat.

After a while, Father gave up.

"He's starting to resent it, just like Jong did," Ah Lee warned Father.

Father looked worried, but he said, "He'll get over it."

Ah Lee sighed. "That's what you said about Jong."

Finally it was time to leave. With the others, we carried our bedding and suitcase down to the wharves. I stopped short when I first saw the ship. It looked as big as our whole village and all the village's fields.

I was so amazed, I forgot to be angry at Father. "It's so huge," I said.

Father pointed to the strange English words. "You can have your next English lesson. That says it's the S.S. *China*."

Father nudged me along. "It's a big ocean," he said, nodding toward another dock. "There are even bigger ships." And I saw ships that could have held two of our villages.

Then I looked at all the water. It swept to the horizon. I couldn't see the Golden Mountain at all. "How far do we have to go?" I asked carefully.

Father waved a hand. "That isn't even the ocean yet."

Suddenly all the ships seemed so small. I felt scared as we joined a line of Chinese waiting to board.

Ah Lee was ahead of us. He turned and smiled at Father. "Are you ready for the rattrap?"

Wart Man was with him. "I hate steerage," he said, wiping his neck with a rag. "And in this weather, it's going to be miserable."

Father glanced at me. I think he wanted to reassure me. "Don't listen to them. We've got it easy, compared to your grandfather. When he first went to the Golden

Mountain, all the Chinese were locked inside the hold, even when it was hot. There was little water and no air. My father was one of the lucky ones who left the ship alive. But don't worry. This is a modern ship."

As we waited in line, the ship looked more and more like a metal prison. When we finally boarded, sailors guided us way below the top deck. The hot, moist air surrounded us like glue. I smelled years of stale sweat.

Our compartment was lined with bunk beds that were crammed together. The sleeping room back in the building in Hong Kong seemed spacious now.

In the compartment, voices echoed loudly and there were people everywhere. The first-timers just stood there in confusion, but old-time Guests headed for the best spots.

"Keep up with Ah Lee," Father urged me.

I concentrated on following our hurrying friend.

When I reached Ah Lee's side, he had already saved a pair of bunk beds for us. Unfortunately, Wart Man took a bunk below us.

Father lifted my bedding onto a bunk and dumped his on the one above. As I climbed onto my new bed, my heart began to thump with excitement. After Father had settled in, he recognized other Guests who were returning to America. They spoke in many dialects. Some of them I had trouble understanding.

Not all the Guests were stopping in San Francisco. Some

were going even farther east, continuing on to faraway places with strange names like New York or Chicago. They seemed to be going all over America.

I noticed that I was the only boy in the compartment. While we waited for the ship to leave, the other men tried to amuse me. They taught me games with cards and dominoes. They told me some of the old stories from China.

Wart Man warned me, "Don't get a swelled head. You're only getting this attention because there aren't many children over there."

I didn't care. It was nice to be everyone's pet for a while.

"He reminds me of my grandchildren," Ah Lee said. "I was hoping to get to know them when I retired."

He sounded sad. I rehearsed my question inside my head until I was confident I could say it. "If you retired, why are you leaving?" I asked him.

Ah Lee lay on his side, pillowing his head on his bent arm. "Some bandits had other ideas."

Wart Man laughed. "So they stripped you clean. All those years of hard work were wasted, and now you have to start over."

Ah Lee raised his hands in resignation. "At least they let me live. And I suppose you're taking this voyage for your health," he snapped.

Wart Man shook his head. "My family's worse than bandits. They just can't seem to hold on to money. It's always spend, spend, spend. Without the Golden Mountain, we'd be fighting the pigs for slops."

"If I didn't have the Golden Mountain, we'd all be battling right next to you," Ah Lee admitted.

Suddenly the ship began to throb. Was it sinking?

"Here we go," Father said. While most of the Chinese looked sad, he seemed almost happy. He wanted to get to America as much as everybody else wanted to stay in China.

Ah Lee took out a piece of paper. Carefully he unfolded it and began to study it. Every now and then, he put it down and closed his eyes. His lips hardly moved as he murmured names softly.

I tried to peek at the paper. "What are you reading?"

Ah Lee gave me an embarrassed smile. "This has got all the facts about my home. Now that I'm older, it's harder to remember things."

Wart Man had taken out his own sheet of notes. "Better not let the Americans catch you with that. They'll send you back to China for sure."

Ah Lee tapped the side of his head. "By the time the trip's done, it'll all be in here."

Other men in the room had also begun to study their own notes. "We should start preparing too," Father said.

Wart Man rattled his paper. "Your boy's too young, and he stammers. He's going to get you kicked out of America for sure."

"He's fine," Father boasted.

Wart Man gave a snort. "When he's calm. But when he gets nervous, he stutters. And you know the Americans. They'll do everything to upset him during the interrogation."

"What d-d-do they do when they test you?" I asked, suddenly alarmed. "Do they h-hit you? Do th-they torture you?"

Wart Man stopped reading for a moment. "No, but they'll make you feel like you've been tortured by the time they're through. They want to throw you off and force you into making a mistake. They'll shoot questions at you like bullets from a machine gun. When they're finished, you'll wonder if you really are yourself."

"You'll be fine," Father assured me.

Wart Man brought his hand down like an executioner's sword. "Five minutes with the Americans and he'll be a miserable wreck. He won't be able to answer a thing. And then you'll both be back in China, rooting for garbage with the pigs."

Hopeless

QUESTION: *What was the trip like?*

POP: *My father kept me pretty busy studying for the test. I had to get ready for Angel Island.*

As I lay in my bunk, I closed my eyes. Instead of being in a hot, stinky ship, I pretended I was at home again. I tried to tell myself that I was lying beside the pond. But the ground didn't roll there the way it did here. And the air didn't pound with the noise of great engines. I could feel the vibrations travel through the metal and up my bunk. They beat rhythmically, like a gigantic heart. I felt as if I had been swallowed up by a monster—a monster that was carrying me away from China.

All around me, I heard men being sick.

I gave up trying to imagine my village and opened my eyes.

"How are you feeling, boy?" Father asked.

I felt kind of uncomfortable, but not all that bad. "Okay."

Father said I was a natural traveler.

As the day went on, the smells and the heat grew worse. I sweated all the time. "I think I've already forgotten what the sky looks like," I told Father.

He stared at the metal walls. "Then let's remind ourselves."

We left the compartment and moved through narrow hallways. They felt just as hot as the compartment. I'd forgotten the route we had taken to come down here, so we seemed to be in a maze. It took us a while before we found the stairs.

We climbed to a deck at the rear. Smoke was coming from one of the funnels. I didn't care. It was good to see the sun again. Then I looked around. There was nothing but ocean. It made me feel as small as an ant. I was glad I was with Father.

Then I heard laughter. Western men and women were playing a game on a higher deck. "Can we see what they're doing?" I asked Father.

He shook his head. "We're not allowed up there. That's first class."

I saw a Chinese man in Western clothes up there. "Is he a servant?"

"He'd wear a uniform then," Father explained. "He's a passenger. He must be rich." He tilted his head back. "But the same sun shines on us as well as him. Let's enjoy what we have."

I hated going back to the compartment. I felt so trapped there.

"I guess we might as well start studying again too," Father said, sitting beside me on my bunk.

"I'm ready," I said.

Father cleared his throat and nodded at Wart Man. "I'm going to do things a little differently today. I'll start imitating the American officials. Up until now, I've let you take your time answering. But no more. And remember to speak clearly."

I thought over what Wart Man had said about the test. "I'll try."

Father started out with simple questions, like asking me his name and my mother's name. I had to tell him my brothers' names and where they were. Then he wanted the names of my grandparents and where they were buried. I managed all those answers fine.

"Do you have any animals?" Father asked.

"We didn't r-r-r-rehearse that one," I said, surprised.

"I just thought of it," Father said. "And treat me like I'm an official."

"No," I said.

Father corrected me with a frown: "We have chickens."

That threw me off, but I worked hard to speak clearly. "They're not pets," I argued. "They're just food."

"That point doesn't concern the Americans," Father said, and quickly demanded, "Where are they?"

I scratched my head, puzzled. "They're s-s-sort of all over."

Father sighed. "There's a coop for them in the courtyard."

I was really nervous now. "Only at n-n-n . . ." I had to pause before I managed to get out the word "night." I could tell right away that this was the wrong answer.

Father did not give me time to think. He did not even pause, but asked immediately, "Do the chickens lay enough eggs for the family, or do we also have to buy them?"

"Y-yes . . . n-no," I said. I wasn't sure. And my stammer was getting worse.

Father coached me: "Just tell them it wasn't your job."

Bang-bang-bang came questions about our fields and the pond. When I made more mistakes, worry lines creased Father's forehead.

He took some rolled-up socks from the suitcase. "Let's try something else. The Americans are going to give you a set of blocks, so let's pretend that's what these are. You have to arrange them like our village."

That was easy.

"Now tell me who lives in each," he commanded.

I took my time answering so I wouldn't stammer. Father shook his head. "Too slow. They're going to be watching you like hawks. Speak faster." He didn't give me time to catch my breath, but pointed to our house. "How many doors?"

I closed my eyes and squinted as I thought real hard. "One."

Father shook his head in disgust. "No, it's two. A large one and a small one."

"B-but we use the small one most of the time," I said.

"What you say has to match the immigration files," Father said.

He kept firing questions at me. And he shifted from one topic to another. This confused me, but the questions only came harder and faster.

"N-n-no. I mean y-yes." I was feeling so nervous, I began to stutter. I finally broke down. "I g-g-guess I don't know."

"Why don't you?" he demanded. He was relentless. He wouldn't stop questioning me. He didn't seem like my father anymore.

I stammered, "W-w-why are you p-p-picking on me?"

Father looked sorry. "Because that's how the Americans will do it."

Though it was still hot inside the compartment, I suddenly felt very cold. "I'm t-t-tired. Can't I rest?"

Father hesitated as if he wanted to be kind, but Wart

Man said, "Do you think the Americans will stop when he asks them to? They want him to break down just like he's doing right now."

Father reluctantly nodded. "He's right, boy. You have to be tougher. Every Guest has to go through this kind of questioning. Almost every time I've returned from visiting my family, the Americans made trouble for me." And then he started badgering me again, without mercy.

With each new day, the compartment seemed tinier and hotter and stinkier. Sometimes we docked in a port, but we weren't allowed off the boat.

All I could do was study. I'd been fine with my lessons in the village, but when Father acted like the American officials, my memory and my tongue failed me. And that only made him more frustrated and worried.

This was worse than school. The quizzes never stopped here. I could not run away. I could not hide.

And I kept getting worse. After a while, I started to think Wart Man was right. I was going to flunk, and then all sorts of bad things would happen. It wouldn't be just my fault, though. Father should never have asked me to come.

It was too much. What made Father think I could do this? I was too young. And I stuttered. I could feel resentment bubbling inside me like water ready to boil.

Then, one long afternoon, Father asked me the name of my textbook in school. When I told him, he shook his head.

"That's for older children. They'll know you're too young."

"But that's the one I was r-reading," I said.

Father sighed. "Don't tell them anything odd. Give them the name of the book other boys your age were reading."

I was proud of reading the more advanced textbook. "But I was smart enough to d-d-do that," I said.

"You say what I tell you to tell them," Father ordered.

He was so unfair. First he had dragged me from home without telling me the truth about his job or the schooling. Then he had tortured me as an American would. He made me so nervous that I stuttered, and he blamed me when I did. Now he wanted me to lie too, and pretend I was dumb. Something snapped inside me. "No! Why sh-should I?"

"You've got to be firm. Show him who's boss. Make him obey," Wart Man urged Father.

"Shut up!" Ah Lee snapped. "Now we know why your family doesn't want you to stay home."

Father was just as hot and tired as I was. He swung out of his bunk and slammed his feet against the floor. "You'll fail if you don't listen to me."

Tears stung my eyes. "I d-d-don't c-care if they s-send me b-back. I d-don't want to l-live if I have to l-lie."

Father bunched his hands into fists. "Just do what I tell you!" he yelled.

The room had fallen silent. All the men were watching

me, especially Wart Man.

I tried to shout back at Father, but my tongue failed me completely. The frustration made me even angrier and more miserable. Finally I burst into tears.

Father didn't look angry, though, only puzzled. He scratched his head like a boy who had just wrecked a toy and didn't know how to fix it. All he could do was keep saying, in a worried voice, "Stop crying."

As the tears coursed down my cheeks, I again tried to answer, but this time all that came from my open mouth were angry, squawking sounds.

"Don't cry, boy." Father started to reach a hand out to me, but stopped. He slapped his leg in frustration. "I told you not to cry."

I felt so ashamed for weeping like a baby. However, when I tried to stop, I just cried all the more. And the harder I tried to speak, the more I squawked.

Father just stood there looking helpless, but Wart Man looked disgusted. "He's a real Mama's boy, all right."

Father turned on his heel. "I'm going to get some water."

When he had left, Ah Lee knelt beside my bunk and patted me on the shoulder. "Your father doesn't mean it. You've got to be patient."

By then I had some control over my tongue. "W-why?"

Ah Lee glanced around, especially at the curious Wart Man. Then he leaned forward and whispered in my ear, "Your father wouldn't be able to admit it to you, but he's lonely."

I could see Wart Man leaning far out of his bunk, trying to overhear us. I kept my own voice low. "B-b-but he has Yuen."

Ah Lee sighed. "Yuen is a grown man. And Jong . . . Well, it was too much of a shock for him when he came to America. He couldn't adjust to being the son of a servant."

This had been hard for me to accept too. "Jong w-w-was always proud," I said, remembering my brother. "F-f-father should have left him in China. He should have let me stay too. But he cares more about money than he does about us."

"No, it's more than money, boy." Ah Lee gripped the bunk. "Try to understand. A Guest does his best for his family while he's in America. Then he goes home. At first everyone treats him with respect. But it doesn't take long before he realizes his own wife and family are foreigners to him." He looked sad, as if he were talking about himself as well. "They don't need you any more than they need an extra basket. All they really need is your money."

I thought of Father in the village. He'd been an outsider to his own clan. It must have been even worse to be one to his family. "H-he d-doesn't need me, though. Y-you h-heard him. M-most of the t-time, I'll be in school."

"But the time you'll be with him will be precious." Ah Lee shifted his weight on his knees, trying to get more comfortable. "A Guest spends most of his life away from his family. He never gets to watch his children grow up. Before he knows it, he's a grandfather. Suddenly he's a stranger to a whole new generation. For all our sacrifices, we don't feel all that Chinese. We don't even feel like fathers. It's just plain lonely being a Guest."

I had a whole jumble of thoughts, but I took my time and spoke carefully. "So Father got t-tired of being alone?"

Ah Lee nodded as he gave up kneeling and rose to a squat. "He wanted to be a good father to your brother, but he just didn't know how. So he did everything wrong." He patted my arm. "You're his second chance. He's determined to do things right with you. Just be patient."

Wart Man made a disgusted noise. Apparently he overheard us. "You shouldn't be telling him this," he said. "What he needs is a spanking. That's the way my father raised me."

"And look how you turned out," Ah Lee shot back over his shoulder. "Sour as a lemon." He turned to me again. "Your father wanted to let you stay at home longer. But the Americans may not give him any more time. We hear they're going to make the immigration laws even tougher. He wasn't sure he could get you in if he waited any longer."

I wiped my face on my sleeve. "It was either n-now or never?"

Ah Lee nodded. "He didn't want to risk it. No one wants to die lonely." Then he returned to his bunk.

I did a lot of thinking before Father returned with a cup of water for me. "Are you thirsty, boy?" he asked shyly. When I stared at his hand, he shifted his feet uncomfortably. "What's wrong?"

"You're using your l-left hand," I said wonderingly.

Embarrassed, Father switched the cup to his right hand. "I forget when I get upset."

I stared at him in amazement. So he'd been left-handed when he was young too! "Th-thank you." I remembered to put out my own right hand when I took the cup. "D-did you get hit too?"

Father rubbed the side of his head sympathetically. "All the time, when I was your age. I thought it had gotten slapped out of me after all these years."

"Did you st-st-stutter too?" I asked.

"No, so I guess I had it easier than you." Father leaned against the bunk. "On the day I came home, your hand was hurting. Did Uncle Jing hit you for stuttering or using your left hand?"

I kept sipping the water even after I wasn't thirsty anymore. I wanted to think carefully about what to say. I rehearsed it over and over in my mind while Father waited patiently. "For both. He said he was just following your orders."

Father winced as if he had been slapped. "No, no. I wanted you to speak clearly, but I didn't want you to get hit when you didn't." He shook his head. "That's my fault. I should have been clearer."

I let that sink in. "You didn't tell Uncle to h-hit me?"

Father straightened. "Of course not."

"B-but you get so upset when I stutter," I said.

Father raised his eyebrows in surprise. "I wasn't really upset with you. I'm worried about what the Americans will do to you."

"So . . . y-you're not actually mad at me when I stammer?" I asked cautiously.

"No," Father said. Then he hesitated. "What about you? Are you still angry at me?"

I shook my head. "No, not really. Or maybe just a little."

Father scratched his cheek. "But you started to act just like Jong did. He resented it almost from the first. He hardly ever spoke to me. And on the rare times when he did, he was insolent."

"W-why . . ." I paused until I was sure I could get the words out clearly. "Why did you bring me? Was it just so I could earn more money?"

"It was more than that, boy." Father looked down at the floor uncomfortably. "We were both in our forties when your mother found out she was pregnant with you. It was such a surprise. We never expected to have any more children. You were our miracle baby."

I glanced at Ah Lee and thought about what he had said. Maybe Father had seen me as his second chance. He could be a parent, finally, to the last of his children.

Once again, Father misunderstood my silence. "I guess I was being selfish," he mumbled. After a moment, he dipped into his things and took out a small, wrinkled paper bag. "I was saving this to celebrate with when we reached San Francisco. It's not much, but I think we need it now." In his nervousness, he forgot himself again and started to use his left hand to open the bag. When he realized this, he drew it back.

I just grinned. "Don't worry. I'm not going to hit you."

He nodded. We shared the same kind of tormentors. That gave us a bond.

Trusting me, he used his left hand to open up the bag. Inside were candied strips of coconut.

I got my box and opened the latch. Father saw the painted toy top.

"I gave you that when I came back this last time," he said, pleased.

I spoke slowly. "I said I would keep my treasures in here."

Father nodded at some colored pebbles. "But those are just rocks."

"They're from our fields," I said. Then I unwrapped the rag from around some preserved salted plums.

"Mother made these. Would you like one?"

"Yes," he said. "Let's have a party."

The coconut made a lump in my cheek. Father moved the plum in his mouth so that it made a bump on his face too.

I laughed at the sight. "Can we start over?"

Father smiled. "Let's."

San Francisco

QUESTION: *Were you glad when the trip was over?*

POP: *I guess, but I was a little scared too. Because of what could happen. Still, nothing beat that first sight of San Francisco.*

July 31, 1922

One day led to another. I didn't like the smelly ship. And after a while, I didn't enjoy the deck anymore. All I could do was sit on the hot metal.

But the thing I hated the most was the studying. Still, bit by bit, I'd gotten less and less rattled. I usually had the answer right away. Most of the time I spoke clearly. However, I still stuttered at other times. That worried Father as much as it did me. He didn't scold me anymore. He knew I was trying my best.

Poor Ah Lee, though, kept making mistakes. Father and I felt sorry for him, so we helped quiz him. After a while, I didn't need to look at his crib sheet to correct him.

For the tenth time that afternoon, I told him, "Excuse me, Ah Lee, but it's a p-peach tree outside your bedroom window."

Ah Lee slapped his forehead and sighed sadly. "You know my home better than I do," he said. However, he never frowned for long. He compared my height to his. "Maybe you can pretend to be me too."

"I just hope I can get in as m-me." I bit my lip. I'd almost managed to say the whole sentence without a mistake. What was going to happen with the Americans?

Suddenly Father held up a hand. "Quiet, boy." Then he turned and said to the other men, "Silence. Listen."

From far away, I heard a bird calling. It was not a pretty sound at all. Instead, it was high, shrill, demanding. However, the men grew excited.

Ah Lee could hear it too. "It's a seagull."

Wart Man leaned his head to the side. "I hear another one."

So did I.

"We're getting close to shore," Father explained. He looked happy. Even in China, I had never seen him this happy.

Ah Lee swung his legs over the side of his bunk. He

tried to wave his arm, but the aisles were too narrow and he hit the next bunk instead. "Let's go on deck."

Father and I got on our feet. All around me, other men were sliding from their bunk beds. Only Wart Man stayed where he was.

Ah Lee poked his side. "Aren't you coming?" he asked.

Wart Man put his head in his hands. "Once I'm in San Francisco, I'll have to work like a dog. I'm going to lie on my bunk for as long as I can. Besides, I've had a bellyful of that awful city."

"We're better off without that sour man," Ah Lee said.

The hallway was crowded. Everybody was too excited to talk. All I could hear was the shuffling of many feet. It sounded like a giant centipede.

A breeze brushed my cheeks as we climbed the stairs. It felt as cool and soft as Mother's hand.

"It's still so hot in the rest of the ship," I whispered to Father.

"The heat must be trapped inside," Father explained in a low voice.

All around the ship, the waves rose and fell. The swells reminded me of the rolling hills at home. It was as if someone had copied them in green glass.

And the open air was now so much cooler and drier than at home. My Western clothes did not stick to me as they had earlier in the voyage.

Everyone was on one side of the ship, trying to glimpse land. The sailors were also on deck, looking for San Francisco.

Father put me on his shoulders. I felt so tall that I was almost dizzy.

On the horizon I saw a dark smear. As the ship cut through the swells, the smear grew. It looked like a long golden worm now. However, the land looked so dead compared to home. I felt disappointed. "Where's the grass? W-where are the trees?" I asked Father.

"In China, it's the rainy season," Father explained, "but here it's the dry season." His hand traced an invisible horizontal line. "You're going to be seeing a whole new city. Sixteen years ago—that was before you were born—a lot of it fell down in an earthquake. And what that didn't destroy, a big, big fire did."

My eyes widened. Now there was something else to be scared of. "Were you in it?"

Father leaned on the railing. "No, I was coming back from China, so I was still in the ship. We got tumbled all around that morning. But it was really strange when we sailed into the harbor. Everywhere there were ruins. And the smoke and dust were still in the air."

"It was the only time you didn't have trouble when you landed," Ah Lee said.

"They hadn't brought in the duplicate records yet,"

Father agreed, "but it took an act of Heaven to make it easy for me."

"M-maybe they'll lose our records this time too," I suggested hopefully.

"All these years, I've prayed for money," Ah Lee said. "I should have really been praying for another earthquake."

As we strained to catch our first sight of San Francisco, Ah Lee began to talk about his home. He was so happy when he spoke about the houses and his friends and about his life here.

When we entered the mouth of the bay, the ship rose and dropped abruptly. "We just crossed the Golden Gate," Father said.* The water was suddenly calmer here.

To the south lay a big brick building that Father said was an American fort. Then we passed by an island Father called Alcatraz. Beyond it lay the real San Francisco. There were so many tall buildings. Father knew every one of them and had stories about them.

The city looked so strange, and yet my family's roots ran deep here. I thought back to the Ching Ming, when we had cleaned my grandparents' graves. The Americans thought that Father and I were just like weeds. They wanted to rip us from the Golden Mountain.

I wouldn't let that happen.

* The bridge had not yet been built across the Golden Gate, the mouth of San Francisco Bay.

Angel Island

QUESTION: *What did you think of America when you first got here?*

POP: *That was Angel Island, and it felt like a prison. But I hadn't done anything wrong. Then I met some of the other guys. Some of them had been stuck there for months. It made me even more scared.*

We switched over to a smaller boat that chugged across the water. There were some Asian men on it, but they didn't dress like Chinese. Father said they were Japanese. There were other men who looked like Westerners. Father told me they were probably Russians.

There were also a few Chinese women. They must have been in another part of the ship.

"There are women trying to get into America," I said hopefully to Father. If women were here, maybe Mother and Sister could join us somehow.

"America will only let you in if you are the wife of a scholar or a merchant," Father explained. "I'm only a houseboy."

Though the water was calmer in the bay, there were still swells. The boat felt them more than the big ship had.

Across the bay, San Francisco looked so beautiful. I would have liked to walk its streets at least once and see the sights up close. But this might be as much as I would ever see.

Ah Lee wasn't looking at the view, but at something in one of his hands. When Father and I sidled over to him, we saw a folded-up sheet of paper.

"Haven't you torn up your notes yet?" Father whispered to him in alarm.

Ah Lee was trying to hold his hat on his head with his free hand. "I will. I just want one last look at them."

"They're a bomb waiting to go off," Father warned.

Though it was sunny, it was cold on the water. Some men were wearing only thin cotton clothes from China. They shivered now in the brisk wind blowing across the bay. Even in my heavy Western clothes, I felt the chill.

For the first time, I was glad I had a new suit. Father had been right. Suddenly I felt proud of how smart Father was.

Next to us, a young man had turned green and was

looking around uncertainly.

A Western guard growled something, but when the young man failed to understand, the guard snatched him by his waistband and hoisted him into the air. Then he helped the man lean over the railing. It was a late case of seasickness.

Behind us were the buildings of San Francisco. Rising before us were the golden hills. In front of them was a lonely little island. Father said the Americans called it Angel Island.

When the boat docked at the wharf, Father and I followed the others onto the shore. Planks thumped under my feet. America felt different from China. I started to wobble. Father caught me with a laugh. "You've still got your sea legs. You're used to adjusting to the motion of the waves."

In front of us stood a big building, with palm trees around it. Father said it was the main building for the Western officials. To our left was a hospital. Smaller buildings were scattered around. The Western guards lived in those.

They all looked like big boxes. Some were two stories high. Their walls seemed so bare compared to Chinese ones. Each of them was painted white. In China, white is the color of mourning and funerals. The buildings looked like coffins wrapped in funeral cloths.

Father pointed to a two-story building on a hill behind the main building. "We'll stay in that place," he said.

With strange snarls, the guards separated the passengers. The women were in one group, and the Japanese and the Russians in two separate clumps.

The Chinese men made up the biggest group, though. We were taken to the hospital first. When we went inside, the bare walls seemed so cold, so odd. Inside a big room stood a Westerner in a white mourning robe. He looked very solemn.

"Is this a funeral for someone?" I whispered to Father.

"He's a doctor," Father said. "He wants to see if we're sick."

I didn't want to take off my clothes for the Westerner, so Father went first to show me it was all right. When I finally undressed, the Westerner poked and prodded but said I was all right. However, another man was sick. He was taken away and put into quarantine.

At least I'd passed one exam.

The Westerners took us to the buildings where we would sleep. Wart Man was the first in line. He began to climb the path up the rising slope. I wished I could be like him. He seemed able to handle anything.

The bars on all the windows scared me. The hospital

had been strange enough. But this place seemed like it was even stranger.

Faces filled the windows on the first floor. Chinese men and women stared at us through the bars. I felt as if I were being sent to jail, though I had done nothing wrong.

A boy grinned down at me. "Fresh meat!" he called. "Welcome to the Land of the Golden Mountain." And he cackled. His voice drifted to me as I labored up the road.

Other men inside called greetings to friends they recognized.

It was dim inside when we entered. I felt as if I were walking into the throat of a giant wooden beast. And its belly was a strange, large room. Metal poles ran from the floor to the ceiling. They supported rows of bunk beds. Each bunk had three beds stacked one over the other. Wet clothes hung from strings, like flags. The room was so crowded, it was dim. It stank like the ship too.

Bored men sat or lay on the bunks. A couple of them were playing a game, using Western cards with funny symbols.

Wart Man immediately headed for the bunks. He moved sideways because the aisle was so narrow. The others fanned out. "Here, boy," Father said, slinging our suitcase onto a bunk bed. I put my box on a top bunk and clambered up after it. Chinese words were carved into the wooden wall next to the bunk.

I looked down at Father, who was unpacking. "Someone wrecked the walls."

Father only glanced at the words. "It's a poem."

My mouth moved slowly as my finger traced the carving:

> *"Winter gives way to spring.*
> *One year gives way to another.*
> *Hope gives way to hope.*
> *In this wooden tower, worry poisons me."*

"What happened to the poet?" I asked.

A boy next to me said, "They say he hanged himself." It was the boy I had seen at the window.

I turned to look at him. The boy lay upon his back, staring up at the bunk over his head.

"W-why?" I asked.

"I heard he failed the exam and they were going to send him home," the boy said. "He couldn't face his family, because they were going to be ruined. I've been here so long that suicide sounds like a good idea."

Suddenly I got nervous, and that made my tongue trip over itself again. "How . . ." I paused to regain control of it. "H-how l-long have you been here?"

"Two years. They keep asking the same questions and I keep giving the same answers, but nothing makes them happy. They won't let me into America or send me back until they're sure one way or another," he said gloomily. He rolled over suddenly, presenting his back to me.

I felt a chill and looked around the room. There were many poems carved on the walls. What had happened to the poets? And what had happened to their poor families?

How long was I going to be stuck here?

Failure

QUESTION: *What happened to some of the others you were with?*

POP: *It was real bad. They got sent back.*

That first night, I closed my eyes and tried to pretend I was back home again. But I'd grown used to the ship's engines. Instead, here there was the odd rhythmic sound of the bay water lapping at the island's edges.

And then I began to hear sobbing, at first from one man, then from another.

I hardly slept at all. For centuries, Chinese had had to wait for exams in order to get government jobs. I wondered if they had felt as anxious as I did.

Wart Man was the first to be interrogated. He came back looking almost ready to cry.

"How did you do?" Father asked him.

"What do you think?" Wart Man said, but his mouth was more sour than normal. He shuffled away.

I thought of the poet who had died. Father must have been thinking the same thing. "We'll have to keep an eye on him," he whispered to me.

I nodded.

Then Ah Lee left, and came back even faster than Wart Man had. He was clutching his head.

I stared at him, worried. "Did you forget the peach tree outside your window?"

He gave a little moan. "Worse. They found my notes."

"I told you to tear them up," Father said. "Why didn't you listen to me?"

"I know, I know," Ah Lee groaned, rocking back and forth, "but I'm too old for this. I don't remember so good. I couldn't pass the exam on my own."

He looked so sad that I felt sorry for him. I tried to point out one blessing: "At least you'll go home to your family."

Ah Lee looked ready to cry. "They won't welcome me. This is a real disaster. We'll lose the house and land and . . . and everything."

Father was more practical. "What will you do?"

Ah Lee shrugged. "Like I said, fight the pigs for scraps until I save up enough to try again."

He'd scared me so badly that my tongue felt as if it were made of wood: "It w-w-w . . ." Finally I gave up.

Father began to look as anxious as Ah Lee. Would my memory and tongue fail me when it was my turn?

My stomach tightened. Every moment I spent on Angel Island, I drew closer to the exam.

Could I pass it? I still didn't know.

Waiting

QUESTION: *What was it like on Angel Island?*

POP: *Some things were funny. Some were scary. Some were embarrassing. Mostly it was boring. It was wait and wait for your test.*

The next morning I started to study on my own. I already knew the facts, but I went over them again.

Breakfast was in another room. The food was cooked and served by other Chinese. They had already passed the test and had been hired by the Westerners. It was hard to cook for so many people. The rice was mushy, and the vegetables were oily from too much grease. The chicken was tough and overcooked. The food was as bad as the ship's.

I missed Mother's cooking. Everything she cooked was just right.

As bad as the food was, some of the men wolfed it down. One of them told me he had never had so much meat. He had been very poor in China, so he had meat only once a year, at New Year's. That was when his clan cut up a pig and handed out pieces.

There was more study after breakfast. Then a lot of men and boys got off their bunks. Father slid off his too. "It's exercise time. Let's go. We only get to do this every seven days."

We were allowed outside, in a space near the building. A fence ran around the sides. It looked like a net, but the strands were metal.

I enjoyed the fresh air. Golden hills surrounded the island. Houses dotted the hills like beads. All too soon we had to go back inside.

I wondered just how long I was going to have to wait. Even though I was scared of the test, I wished I could be done with it one way or the other. I asked Father when the Westerners would examine me.

"Whenever they feel like it," he sighed. "It could be tomorrow. It could be next week or next month. Who knows?"

And who knew when they would stop quizzing me?

The next five days were a lot like the others. I was stuck in my bunk except for meals. Then, on the sixth day, two

Westerners came in. One of them filled in the carved poems with some odd white stuff. The other slapped new paint over the filled-in patches.

As I watched the poems disappear, I felt sorry for the poets. It was as if they had never been.

The Westerners wanted to wipe away all traces of us.

The Test

QUESTION: *Was the exam hard?*

POP: *It wasn't easy. But I knew what to say, so it didn't take long.*

August 7, 1922

Eight days later, I hesitated at an open doorway. This was it. The room was bare except for a table and four chairs. Behind the table were three strangers. Two of them were Westerners and one was Chinese. Not even the Chinese man looked friendly.

They hadn't let Father come with me. They would interrogate him next. I felt afraid.

"Come in, boy," the Chinese man ordered.

My heart felt as if it were running around inside my chest, just like a hen chasing a worm. My feet felt as if they were glued to the floor.

When I stayed in the doorway, the Westerners began to look angry. Had I already failed the exam? Would they jail me here for two years like that boy? Would they send me and my whole family back to China? If that happened, I didn't know if I would want to live either.

"Come in," the Chinese man insisted in a louder voice.

Cautiously, I stepped into the room. My Western shoes squeaked loudly on the floor.

"Take a seat," the Chinese man ordered. He waved a hand at the unoccupied chair in front of the table.

I sat down hesitantly on the very edge of the seat. Fat folders of papers lay scattered across the table. I wondered how many of those folders were about our family.

A Westerner in the middle was examining a folder. His face was all red, which made him look even angrier than the others. He picked up a photograph that we had sent to Father. He studied it and then examined my face from all angles. He pursed his lips the way Uncle Jing did when he graded my calligraphy.

When the Westerner finally spoke, he sounded as if he were barking and growling.

The Chinese man listened. When the Westerner was finished, he said, "The inspector was ordering you to tell the truth, boy."

My mouth was suddenly so dry. I tried to answer, but

my voice came out as a croak. So I just nodded my head.

Through the interpreter, the inspector asked, "Who are you?"

For a moment my mind went blank. I could feel everyone's eyes on me. I couldn't breathe. I was going to fail too, just like my friends.

My thoughts whirled around inside my mind like dead leaves. I saw Uncle and his bamboo rod. I remembered my laughing classmates. Mother would be frowning. Father would be angry.

No, no. When I thought that, my tongue always started tripping. *Don't think about them,* I told myself. *Just think about the question. The question. What was it? Oh yes, my name.*

"Yep Gim Lew," I said, slowly and clearly.

The other Westerner wrote something down on a pad. I tried to peek, but the words looked just like squiggles to me.

"How old are you?" they asked through the interpreter.

"Ten," I said clearly. I felt good after winning another little victory.

"Do you know when you were born?" they asked.

I felt the words pour into my mouth, but I didn't try to rush. When I hurried, my tongue never could keep up. "Second year of the Republic, tenth month, twenty-eighth day."

"Who told you that was when you were born?" they asked.

"My mother," I said.

The strangers wanted to know all sorts of things about my family. Where was my mother? What was her name? Who else was living in our house? Every now and then, they looked at the folder.

The questions came faster and faster.

How many brothers did I have? Had I seen any of them?

I told them I had seen Yuen and Jong.

They showed me a photo of Jong. "Is he married?" the stranger asked.

I wanted to tell them he was too young yet, but I kept my answer simple: "No."

Where were my other brothers?

I explained that they were in Penang.*

They gave me blocks. I arranged them like the houses in my village.

Where was my school? Who was my teacher? Did he have family? How many rooms did my house have? Did I sleep at home? Did anyone else sleep in the same room? How many other children went to school? On and on they went.

They shot questions at me like arrows. They tried to upset me. They were hoping for a mistake. They wanted any excuse to keep me from setting foot in America and for tearing out the roots of my entire family.

But I wouldn't let them!

* In what is now Malaysia

I did not have time to be afraid anymore. I was fighting for Mother and Sister, for Sister-in-Law and my nephew. And for all my brothers.

Their questions didn't rattle me. My memory was holding up. I knew the answers. Father had trained me well.

I was battling not only the strangers, but my own clumsy tongue. So far, I was winning against both.

Maybe I was going to pass the test.

The Future

QUESTION: *Do you miss China?*

POP: *I did. But that was a long time ago. This is home
now.*

I didn't stutter. I didn't make a mistake either. After all
that worrying, the interview had been short. Father was
pleased. He said I'd done well because I had studied so
hard.

Even so, we had to wait. Thirteen days later, the
Westerners said we could leave the island.

As we were packing up our things, Ah Lee wrote a
note. His hand moved slowly and awkwardly. He didn't
seem used to writing.

"Here's my cousin's address. Tell him I didn't make it,"
Ah Lee said.

Father took the note and folded it up carefully. "I'm sorry."

Ah Lee just shrugged. "As soon as I scrape the fare together, I'll return. You just wait. We'll be having tea in San Francisco one day." He was trying to put a brave face on the disaster.

"I'll look forward to it," Father promised, and then coughed politely to address Wart Man, who was lying on his bunk, facing toward the city. "Is there any message you want me to take?"

Wart Man kept staring at the window. "Tell my uncle that I'm glad I failed the test. I hate doing laundry. You can't wash dirty clothes without the filth rubbing off on you." He gave us his uncle's address.

Ah Lee reached across the aisle and slapped Wart Man's back. "At least we'll keep each other company on the return trip."

Wart Man shoved Ah Lee's hand away. "My family's in as much of a mess as yours. So what have you got to be so cheerful about?"

Ah Lee looked a little afraid, but he was trying to make the best of things. "It's like the boy said: we get to go back to China."

"And eat with the pigs now. I hate China," Wart Man grumbled.

"You didn't seem to like living there," Father agreed.

"I hate America worse," Wart Man snapped. He turned his back on all of us. "I just hate my whole life."

Ah Lee chuckled sadly. "He's a regular lemon man."

Wart Man covered his ears with his hands. "And the final punishment is having to listen to you all the way back."

Father squeezed Ah Lee's shoulder. "Don't tease him too much," he whispered.

Ah Lee put his hands upon his chest indignantly. "But Lemon Man's not happy if he doesn't have something to complain about."

I thought of the strange streets and people across the water, and I felt scared. Every day would bring new unofficial little tests. Could I pass them too?

"Come on, boy." Father picked up our suitcase and all our bedding. I got my box and followed him toward the door.

The boy in the bunk next to mine tried to kick me as I passed. "It's not fair. It's not fair," he said, beginning to cry.

I turned to wave to Ah Lee and Wart Man, but they were both lying in their bunks, looking the other way. I hoped they would be all right.

When I stepped outside, I blinked and stood in the bright sunlight. A seagull hovered in the air with wings outspread. It was riding the wind.

"You did well, boy," Father said in a low voice. "I'm proud of you."

"Thank you," I said clearly, without tripping over my tongue.

I trailed after Father. He walked with long strides, eager to get to the boat that would take us to San Francisco. His feet thumped rapidly on the planks of the creaking dock.

Somewhere on the bay, the bell of a buoy rang a greeting. A friendly breeze suddenly swept in. It wrapped itself around me like a cool, welcome blanket. The smell of the sea was strong, but pleasant. A line of black birds with long outstretched necks skimmed the waves. Straight as arrows, they were shooting over the water toward San Francisco, pointing the way for me.

My blood, my American blood, began to race through my veins and arteries. I felt as if they were the strands of a net that was drawing me and my Chinese bones straight toward that unknown land.

Father nodded his head toward San Francisco. "There's your new home, boy."

Home.

As I followed him onto the boat, I almost skipped. I kept my eyes on the gleaming buildings.

More About Chinese American Immigration

Angel Island was where my father first met America, and it was where he took his leave of it: when he died, my family said good-bye to him there. So it is a fitting place to end this book.

My father never returned to China. For more details about his life in San Francisco, I would refer readers to my autobiography, *The Lost Garden*. But in that book I didn't really get to write about how much my father liked American sports. At one time he was even a playground director who coached children in everything from baseball to tennis and volleyball. However, his true passions were basketball and football. (When my wife, Joanne Ryder, met him for the first time, he insisted that she feel the bump on the bridge of his nose—the souvenir of a youthful football game in which his nose had been broken. It had never been set properly.) My father and his friends played all the sports their white counterparts did, but because of prejudice and discrimination, they usually did so separately, within Chinatown. I'm writing about that generation in a forthcoming book, *Dragon Road*, which describes how some of my father's friends joined a professional Chinese American basketball team that barnstormed around America. My niece, Dr. Kathleen S. Yep, is a college professor in Southern California. She is writing a book about Chinese American teenagers in the 1930s and 1940s whose basketball teams served as surrogate families. Her research is based on oral histories from female and male former basketball players in San Francisco's Chinatown.

My father's mother died after the Communists took over mainland China in 1948. Though she had escaped to then-British-controlled Hong Kong, she insisted on returning to her village in mainland China to perform certain rituals, and she never returned to Hong Kong. My grandfather, who was in America, did not live many years past her death. My aunt wound up emigrating to Vancouver.

I undertook this book as a complement to the Golden Mountain Chronicles, for my father was a Chinese American raised in China. I should stress that this is a work of fiction, but it is based on exhaustive interviews in the immigration files, and additional sources such as oral histories of former Angel Island detainees.

My niece Kathleen found the immigration files while doing some family research at the National Archives. These files were full of papers over eighty years old, containing dry information such as dates of arrival and departure. Yet these papers were treasures to our family. Through them, we saw my father's clunky handwriting as a child, and we learned about our family's lives in San Francisco by reading letters from Caucasian employers vouching for them. In addition, the files had immigration photos of my grandfather spanning many years. Before then, our family had never seen photos of him or met him. In these files, he spoke to us through images and transcriptions.

The research was supplemented by my memories of conversations with my father. Among other things, he had once mentioned that he had been left-handed as a boy and had also stuttered. This surprised me, because there was no trace of either by the time I was born. There were other comments my father had made that came back to me as I worked on this book. For example, he had mentioned that he remembered the houses in Macao being pink. (I think he meant the houses in a wealthy area of Macao called Penha Hill. These fancy buildings would impress a small boy from a rural village.) I especially recall how my father spoke with relish about his boyhood treat of sugarcane.

The transcripts from interrogations at Angel Island also served as a source of other research. A sketch of a typical

Cantonese house in an architecture book matches squarely with descriptions given by my family. An anecdote in Harry Franck's *Roving Through Southern China* about the prevalence of bandits and pirates in the region explained why my grandfather and father had taken an indirect but safer route to Hong Kong.[1]

It might also be useful for the reader to have a brief history of Chinese immigration in general and of Angel Island specifically.

My family comes from a district in China called Sun Ning, which was renamed Toisan after the Chinese revolution of 1911. Toisan is a poor area of Kwangtung Province in southern China, so its people have had to travel to other lands to find work. It's estimated that there are approximately 1.3 million Chinese in eighty countries who can currently trace their ancestry back to this one district. The people of Toisanese descent overseas now outnumber the million inhabitants of Toisan.

Chinese had been entering the United States since before 1849.[2] However, the Gold Rush in California brought them in large numbers, despite the risky voyage. The rich goldfields inspired them to name America the Land of the Golden Mountain. Many of them left their families in China, where their wives, like my grandmother,

[1] Franck, *Roving Through Southern China*, p. 313.
[2] Tchen, *New York Before Chinatown*.

110

were responsible for raising the children and running the household.[3] Even though the men spent most of their lives in America, they called themselves Guests of the Golden Mountain. However, in the goldfields they met prejudice, discrimination, and physical violence. My novels *The Serpent's Children* and *Mountain Light* describe the desperation that drove these men to the United States and the violence they met here.

Sometime during the Gold Rush my great-grandfather arrived in California and settled in San Francisco. I wish I knew when he got married and how his wife joined him in America. All I know is that in 1868 she gave birth to my grandfather in San Francisco, which made him an American citizen.

It was during this time that the transcontinental railroad was being built. The western part was completed in 1869 by Chinese immigrants working for the Southern Pacific. I tell some of their stories in *Dragon's Gate*.

When miners could no longer find much gold and the railroad was completed, these resourceful Guests found other work in the American West. It was the Chinese who provided the raw labor to build the California economy. Without them, the West could never have grown as fast as it did. Their labor converted swamps and marshes into

[3] Espiritu, *Asian American Women and Men*; Hsu, *Dreaming of Gold, Dreaming of Home*.

profitable farmland.[4] In the small towns of California, one can still stumble across relics from that time. For example, locals will point to a rock wall and refer to it as "the Chinese wall"—a humble monument to long-vanished builders.

There were strong anti-Chinese feelings from the very beginning of their immigration. In the early 1850s, Chinese, like most nonwhites, were not allowed to vote, become citizens, or testify in court. So as long as there were no whites as witnesses, a white robber could steal from and kill Chinese immigrants without fear of going to trial. A mining tax specifically aimed at Chinese was passed in 1852, and the tax was raised in subsequent years.

Hatred of the Chinese increased into the 1870s, when many laws were passed that not only restricted where Chinese could live and work but also how they could style their hair. The financial panic of 1873 brought ruin to the U.S. economy. Businesses went bankrupt. Banks closed, and depositors found that their money was gone. Many Americans lost their jobs. They blamed the Chinese for their financial troubles. Along with politicians and businesspeople, they lobbied for laws against the Chinese. Mobs attacked and murdered Chinese immigrants and destroyed many little Chinatowns all over the West.

[4] Takaki, *Strangers from a Different Shore*, p. 89.

In the fall of 1881, my grandfather went to China for the first time. It's probable that my great-grandparents wanted him to receive a Chinese education. It's also possible that my great-grandparents were afraid of the violence being directed at Chinese in America. I've written about some of the deadly chaos of that time in *The Traitor*.

Racial hatred eventually led Americans to pass laws that specifically restricted Chinese immigration. The 1875 Page Law limited female Chinese immigration. The Chinese Exclusion Act of 1882 set up even more obstacles for Chinese women, as well as for men, when they tried to enter America.[5] In 1888, with a few exceptions, Chinese were banned altogether from coming to the United States.[6] These laws were designed to prevent Chinese men and women from settling permanently in America or creating families here.[7] Instead, husbands and wives, mothers and sons, sisters and brothers, were kept apart for decades, if not forever.

To enforce these laws, immigration officials began to keep detailed records on Chinese immigrants, including photographs.[8] (To understand just how detailed these records were, try drawing a map of the block on which you

[5] Peffer, *If They Don't Bring Their Women Here.*
[6] Hutchinson, *Legislative History of American Immigration Policy,* 1798–1965, pp. 80–83, 92–94, 101–102, 128–130, 430–433.
[7] Chan, *Asian Americans*, pp. 106–107.
[8] Pegler-Gordon, *American Quarterly* 58: pp. 51–77.

live. List all the people in each house and what they do, and also list all their pets. Then record the births, deaths, and marriages of all your immediate family—including uncles and aunts, parents, brothers, sisters, and grandparents—for three generations and describe what the current living relatives do and where they live. Finally, write down how many windows and doors the houses have and in which direction they face. That will give you some idea how much a Chinese immigrant was expected to know. It was a terrible ordeal for my grandfather, father, and uncles, but it has provided a wealth of information for their descendants.)

By the 1900s, the rural Chinese America had all but vanished. However, the urban Chinese America survived. In cities like San Francisco, Chinese clung to their homes despite anti-Chinese violence. They were kept segregated in their own communities. Laws prevented them from attending schools with other racial groups, barred them from marrying non-Chinese, and even prohibited them from owning land. Because of immigration restrictions targeting Chinese, the surviving Chinatowns were populated mostly by men.

Despite this, Chinese were beginning to sink roots into America. These Chinese Americans saw themselves as bridges between China and America. They hoped to combine and embody the best of both cultures. My novel *Dragonwings* deals with some of that generation.

Two years after my father came to America, in 1924, a new law kept out any immigrant who could not become a citizen.[9] Since it was impossible for an Asian immigrant to become a citizen in the first place, this effectively ended immigration for Chinese as well as for other Asians. However, since my grandfather had been born in America, he was automatically a citizen, and even though his sons had been born in China, they were also American citizens. That made it possible for another of my father's older brothers to come here after my father did.[10] However, my father's mother never came to the United States. My father never saw his home or his mother again.

During the Gold Rush era, Chinese immigrants simply left the ships that carried them from China and walked ashore. However, after the passage of the 1882 Chinese Exclusion Act the Chinese were detained before they could enter America. They were imprisoned in a two-story shed at the end of a wharf belonging to the Pacific Mail Steamship Company (which owned the S.S. *China*, among other ships; later, the line was sold to a group of Chinese Americans and became the China Mail Steamship Company). Sometimes as many as five hundred could be crowded into the shed. While the

[9] Hutchinson, *Legislative History*, p. 188.
[10] Salyer, "Laws Harsh as Tigers," in *Entry Denied*, pp. 76, 83.

interrogations went on, Chinese immigrants could be kept in custody indefinitely.

The Angel Island detention center is often referred to as the Ellis Island of the West, and from 1910 to 1940 most of the 175,000 Chinese immigrants to the United States went there first.[11] This immigration station was expected to handle a flood of European immigrants as well when the Panama Canal opened and connected the Atlantic Ocean with the Pacific. However, by the time that happened, in 1914, Europe was torn by World War I, and European immigrants chose not to make the much longer sea voyage to the West Coast—especially when German U-boats began to make any ship travel dangerous. As a result, 97 percent of the immigrants who passed through Angel Island were Chinese.[12]

Work on the detention center was started in 1905. It was to be built on what had been military property. Surveys were done and plans were drawn, but the Great Earthquake of 1906 stopped the work, as rebuilding San Francisco had become more important.[13]

After visiting his family in China, my grandfather returned to San Francisco on April 19, 1906—one day after the Great Earthquake. At the time, fires would have

[11] Clauss, *Angel Island,* p. 64.
[12] *Ibid.,* p. 60.
[13] *Ibid.*

been destroying what was left of San Francisco. Since local immigration records were lost and the authorities were distracted by other priorities at that time, my grandfather seems to have been processed fairly quickly when he arrived. (Duplicates of the lost records were brought in after that.)

Work on Angel Island resumed in 1907. The immigration station started to process arrivals in October 1908 but was not officially opened until January 21, 1910. Immigrants were ferried straight from the ships to Angel Island. They were each allowed to carry only one suitcase; the rest of their belongings were locked up. Chinese were also separated from other races and other Asian immigrants, and the few Chinese women were kept apart from the men. Husbands and wives were not allowed to see one another, even at meals.[14]

Many of the Chinese who passed through Angel Island compared the barracks to a jail because of the guards and because of their confinement behind fences and barred windows. Crammed together, they lived in large, poorly lit rooms stripped of all furniture except for rows of bunks with beds stacked three high.

There was little privacy. The bathrooms and showers

[14] Lai, Lim, and Yung, *Island*, p. 14; interview with Jeong Foo Louie, an eighty-year-old ex-detainee on Angel Island, August 29, 1976, Angel Island Oral History Project/Combined Asian American Resources Project.

lacked doors for the women and partitions for the men. Individuals washed their laundry by hand and hung it on ropes that were tied to their bunks.

The immigrants were allowed outside only once a week—the women could take a walk under supervision, while the hundreds of men would crowd into a small fenced yard.[15]

Acting Commissioner Luther C. Steward, who was in charge of Angel Island, complained that the barracks were unsanitary. Subsequent officials criticized the facility for other reasons, one of them going so far as to call it "a conglomeration of ramshackle buildings which are nothing but firetraps."[16]

During that thirty-year period of immigration through Angel Island, Chinese could be kept there as long as two years before a decision was made on their status. Jammed together with so many others, they would fight fear, despair, and boredom. The food was so bad that they rioted in the early 1920s. Many of the immigrants at Angel Island created a group that successfully lobbied for better living conditions while they were imprisoned. Members of the San Francisco Chinese community also

[15] Interview with Mrs. Lee, December 14, 1975, Angel Island Oral History Project/Combined Asian American Resources Project; interview with Mrs. Wong, December 15, 1976, Angel Island Oral History Project/Combined Asian American Resources Project.
[16] Clauss, *Angel Island*, p. 60.

protested the immigration process on Angel Island.

There are many poems that detained Chinese men and women carved into the walls over the years.[17] These poems expressed their sadness, hopes, and frustrations.

Even before an electrical fire in August 1940 had destroyed the administration building on Angel Island, the government had decided to switch the immigration facility back to San Francisco. On November 5, 1940, Chinese detainees were moved to an area in southern San Francisco.[18] In 1941, with America's entry into World War II, Angel Island was returned to the military, and the immigration station there was officially closed.

In 1943 the United States repealed all the exclusion acts because it was now an ally of China in the fight against the Japanese during World War II.[19] However, only 105 Chinese immigrants were allowed in each year, and immigrants were still detained on Angel Island until the 1950s. Other immigration laws still made it hard for Chinese to enter America until 1965, when those laws were changed.[20] The effect of all these harsh immigration

[17] Ibid., p. 68.
[18] Lai, Lim, and Yung, *Island*, p. 14.
[19] Hutchinson, *Legislative History*, pp. 264–265. It was said that America's harsh immigration laws against Asians were providing a propaganda subject for the Japanese.
[20] Lai, Lim, and Yung, *Island*, p. 14; Hutchinson, *Legislative History*, pp. 366–379.

laws was to keep the population of San Francisco's Chinatown small and unbalanced. There were relatively few women within San Francisco's Chinese community, and thus the creation of families was delayed. In the face of these challenges, the Chinese in San Francisco still formed a small but vibrant community—the intimate place that I knew as a child and wrote about in *Child of the Owl.*

Today Angel Island is part of the California State Park system and the immigrant detention center is being restored. However, the system lacks the resources to protect and record all of the carved poems on the barracks walls before they wear away. The Angel Island Immigration Station Foundation (www.aiisf.org) is doing its best to save this neglected but significant part of U.S. history. It has created a curriculum guide for teachers of grades three through twelve, and it leads tours for schoolchildren around the detention center. One can reach the detention center by a ferry ride and a short hike.[21]

I owe a word of thanks to Neil Thomsen of the National Archives for his help with immigration files, as well as to Steven Davenport and William Kooliman of the Maritime Museum for their information on the voyage of

[21] Clauss, *Angel Island,* p. 59.

the S.S. *China*. In addition, Albert Cheng and Him Mark Lai, coordinators of the "In Search of Roots" program, offered my niece guidance in locating immigration files. This program is sponsored by the Chinese Culture Foundation of San Francisco (CCF), the Chinese Historical Society of America (CHSA), and the Overseas Chinese Affairs Office in Guangdong Province, People's Republic of China.

Yep Lung Gon, as a young man,
pre-1911, National Archives

Yep Lung Gon, age 51,
1919, National Archives

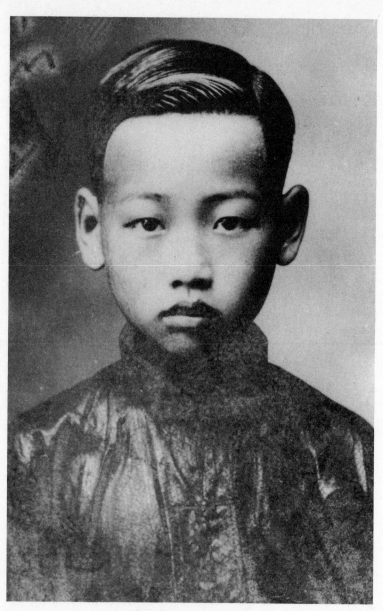

Yép Gim Lew, age 9,
1921, National Archives

Yep Gim Lew, age 10,
1922, Courtesy of the Yep family

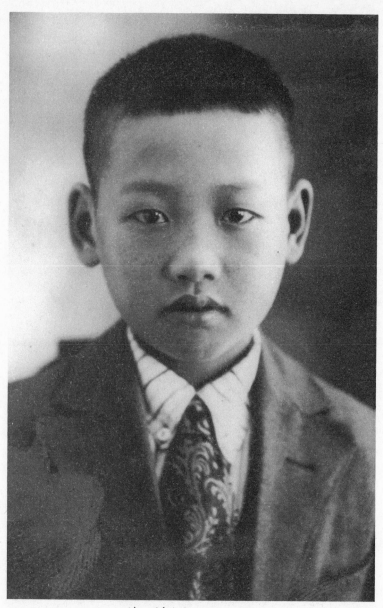

Yep Gim Lew, age 10,
1922, National Archives

Chinese in San Francisco Bay, waiting to be sent to Angel Island,
National Archives

Chinese on S.S. China, before October 1911,
Hawaii State Archives

Angel Island poem,
San Francisco Chronicle

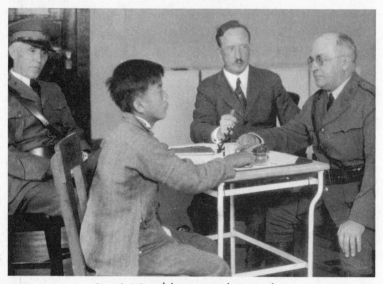

Angel Island interrogation session,
National Archives

Bibliography

Angel Island Oral History Project, sponsored by University of California, Berkeley, Asian American Studies Dept.; funded by California State, Dept. of Parks and Recreation; subjects interviewed by Judy Yung, 1988–1990.

Angel Island Oral History Project/Combined Asian American Resources Project, 1975–1977; subjects interviewed by H. Mark Lai, Genny Lim, and Judy Yung.

Chan, Sucheng, ed. *Entry Denied: Exclusion and the Chinese Community in America, 1882–1943*. Philadelphia: Temple University Press, 1991.

Chan, Sucheng. *Asian Americans: An Interpretive History*. Immigrant Heritage of America. Boston: Twayne, 1991.

Clauss, Francis J. *Angel Island: Jewel of San Francisco Bay*. Menlo Park, CA: Briarcliff Press, 1982.

Espiritu, Yen Le. *Asian American Women and Men: Labor, Laws, and Love*. Thousand Oaks, CA: Sage, 1997.

Franck, Harry A. *Roving Through Southern China*. New York: Century, 1925.

Gee, Jennifer. "Housewives, Men's Villages, and Sexual Respectability: Gender and the Interrogation of Asian Women at the Angel Island Immigration Station." In *Asian/Pacific Islander American Women: A Historical Anthology*, edited by Shirley Hune and Gail Nomura, 90–105. New York: NYU Press, 2003.

Gyory, Andrew. *Closing the Gate: Race, Politics, and the Chinese Exclusion Act*. Chapel Hill: University of North Carolina Press, 1998.

Hammond, Jonathan. "Xiqi Village, Guangdong: Compact with Ecological Planning." In *Chinese Landscapes: The Village as Place*, edited by Ronald G. Knapp, 95–106. Honolulu: University of Hawaii Press, 1992.

Hing, Bill Ong. *Making and Remaking Asian America Through Immigration Policy, 1850–1990*. Stanford, CA: Stanford University Press, 1993.

Hsu, Madeleine Yuan-yin. *Dreaming of Gold, Dreaming of Home: Transnationalism and Migration Between the United States and South China, 1882–1943*. Stanford, CA: Stanford University Press, 2000.

Hutchinson, Edward P. *Legislative History of American Immigration Policy, 1798–1965*. Philadelphia: University of Pennsylvania Press, 1981.

Lai, H. Mark, Genny Lim, and Judy Yung. *Island: Poetry and History of Chinese Immigrants on Angel Island 1910–1940*. Seattle: University of Washington Press, 1991.

Lau, Estelle T. *Paper Families: Identity, Immigration Administration, and Chinese Exclusion*. Durham, NC: Duke University Press, 2006.

Lee, Erika. *At America's Gates: Chinese Immigration During the Exclusion Era, 1882–1943*. Chapel Hill: University of North Carolina Press, 2003.

Lim, Genny, ed. *The Chinese American Experience: Papers from the Second National Conference on Chinese American Studies*. San Francisco: Chinese Historical Society of America, 1984.

Lowe, Felicia. "Carved in Silence." Film, 1988. Lowedown Productions, 565 Alvarado Street, San Francisco, CA 94114. lowedown@aol.com.

Lubhéid, Eithne. "A Blueprint for Exclusion: the Page Law, Prostitution, and Discrimination Against Chinese Women." In *Entry Denied: Controlling Sexuality at the Border*, 31–54. Minneapolis: University of Minnesota Press, 2002.

Peffer, George Anthony. *If They Don't Bring Their Women Here: Chinese Female Immigration Before Exclusion*. Urbana: University of Illinois Press, 1999.

Pegler-Gordon, Anna. "Chinese Exclusion, Photography, and the Development of U.S. Immigration Policy." *American Quarterly* 58, no. 1 (2006): 51–77.

Perkins, Dorothy. "Coming to San Francisco by Steamship." In Lim, *The Chinese American Experience*, 26–33.

Salyer, Lucy E. "'Laws Harsh as Tigers': Enforcement of the Chinese Exclusion Laws, 1891–1924," in *Entry Denied*, edited by Sucheng Chan.

Schwendinger, Robert J. "Investigating Chinese Immigrant Ships and Sailors." In Lim, *The Chinese American Experience*, 16–25.

Soennichsen, John. *Miwoks to Missiles: A History of Angel Island*. Tiburon, CA: Angel Island Association, 2001.

Takaki, Ronald. *Strangers from a Different Shore: A History of Asian Americans*. Boston: Little, Brown, 1989.

Tchen, John Kuo Wei. *New York Before Chinatown: Orientalism and the Shaping of American Culture, 1776–1882*. Baltimore: John Hopkins University Press, 1999.

Wong, K. Scott, and Sucheng Chan, eds. *Claiming America: Constructing Chinese American Identities During the Exclusion Era*. Philadelphia: Temple University Press, 1998.

Yung, Judy. *Unbound Voices: A Documentary History of Chinese Women in San Francisco*. Berkeley: University of California Press, 1999.

WEB RESOURCES

ANGEL ISLAND IMMIGRATION STATION FOUNDATION (AIISF)
AIISF is a nonprofit organization whose mission is to promote a greater understanding of Pacific Coast immigration and its role in shaping America's past, present, and future. In addition to working on preserving the Immigration Station, it provides interpretive programs and educational materials.
www.aiisf.org

KQED ASIAN EDUCATION INITIATIVE: ANGEL ISLAND
This site affiliated with the public broadcasting station for Northern California includes timelines, lesson plans, and photos regarding Angel Island and Chinese immigration.
www.kqed.org/w/pacificlink/history/angelisland

ANGEL ISLAND ORGANIZATION
This site is associated with the California Department of Parks and Recreation and includes a history of the island, archival photographs, and information about visiting Angel Island.
www.angelisland.org/immigr02.html

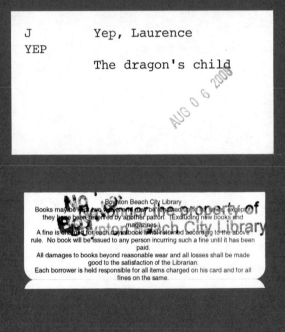